EXIGENT CIRCUMSTANCES

BY ROBERT RAHULA

ALSO BY ROBERT RAHULA

NOVELS*:*
Messieurs
Panamaniac
Island of Misfits
Day Another Paradise In
One Last Fling
Bathhouse Stories
Conversation in a Belgian Bar
All the Yage in Reno
Uninvited Guest

POETRY:
Trigger Points
Dentro Del Corazón Bloqueada
Camino
Migration
I Sing the Body Politic
Wonderland
From Whose Bourn
Poemas Españoles
Expat Poems

SHORT STORIES:
Horror Stories for Children

ANTHOLOGIES:
Half Life
The Essential Dan Landes

EXIGENT CIRCUMSTANCES

First Printing 2018
ISBN 978-0-9994736-7-2

Alma-gator Press
Barcelona • Madrid • La Chorrera

Introduction by Joseph Wambattan:

The character of Dan Landes first appears in Robert Rahula's novel *Island of Misfits*. But in that novel, as in the novel *One Last Fling*, Dan Landes is a peripheral character—an expat retired detective who befriends the main character Ricardo, helping him to solve a murder in the former book, and helping him to commit a murder in the latter. However, in the novel *Bathhouse Stories*, the situation is reversed. The character of Ricardo is relegated to the background, and Dan Landes takes center stage.

Having read and enjoyed so many of Robert Rahula's "sexistential" novels about the bisexual expat Ricardo, I was dismayed to see Ricardo "demoted" to being a secondary character in *Bathhouse Stories*. Yet, as I read the novel, I began to appreciate why Robert Rahula made the shift. Here was Dan Landes, a far more complex and existentially torn character, with a darker past than Ricardo, who could delve into questions regarding justice, law, government and ethics, that were outside of Ricardo's world.

While each of Robert Rahula's nine English novels stands on its own, the characters and locations are consistent from one book to the next, with each book subtly building on the previous books, creating a series of interrelated lives in the tiny town of Villa Rosario. Besides Ricardo and his sexual proclivities, there is Fernando, the corrupt but effective police chief of Villa Rosario; his nephew, Jorge Manuel, the inexperienced police chief of the nearby city of La Chorrera; Jenny, the respected—and lethal—madam of the local brothel; Magali, the reclusive prostitute who works for Jenny and who is loved by both Ricardo and Dan; Miguel, the long-time friend and ex-lover of Ricardo, and owner of Los Cuñados Restaurant in La Chorrera; Marco, the occasional companion to Ricardo; and a host of other characters who inhabit the twin cities of Villa Rosario and La Chorrera. Most importantly, there is Dan Landes—the ex-detective from Los Angeles who uses the indigenous psychedelic drink of ayahuasca to both numb his own pain and increase his crime-solving skills.

It goes without saying that Robert Rahula's books are works of fiction, and his characters are not based on real people, yet he has created a world so real, so inhabitable, that each book is like returning to the town you grew up in—a town full of dark secrets that are uncovered, layer by layer, with each visit.

So come with me and explore this world. If you have read other Robert Rahula books, let me say "welcome home." If this your first Robert Rahula book, then be prepared to delve into the surreal Latino world of expat Dan Landes—a world where, as a brujo once told Dan, "*Una vez un devoto, siempre un devoto.*"

Chapter 1

There was a young man from Thailand...

It was the hotel's third floor housekeeper who found the body that had once been inhabited by the life force known as Khambang Bunyasarn. It was past one p.m., and check-out time was noon. There was a "Do Not Disturb" sign dangling from his doorknob, and Alma Vasquez—which was the housekeeper's name—had already given the guest the benefit of the doubt and had waited until noon before she had first knocked on his door. But there had been no answer. At 12:30 she had gone down to the front desk to confirm that Mr. Bunyasarn was supposed to check out today. Marco, who was working the front desk, checked the reservations. Yes, today was Mr. Bunyasarn's last day. (To be more correct, the previous day had been his last day—as in, last day on earth—but we'll get to that.)

"Damn gringos," Alma thought to herself, but then remembered that Khambang Bunyasarn was Asian. "Damn Asian gringos," she corrected herself and went back up to the third floor. She still had to restock the soft drink machine down the hall from Mr. Bunyasarn's room. She would do that first—that would give him another ten minutes.

But when she came back to his room ten minutes later and knocked again, there was still no answer. She hesitated to open the door with her pass key. She had done that last week and had found a gringo *in flagrante delicto* with a transvestite prostitute. *That* had been an embarrassing day.

She knocked again, this time very loudly. Still no response. She got her pass key out, but then she was reminded again of the sight of that other gringo's fat white ass last week as he was pounding into that bent-over ladyboy prostitute. Alma winced and put the pass key back into her smock pocket and went downstairs to talk to Marco again.

"That gringo in room 323," she asked Marco in Spanish, "has he checked out?"

"He's not a gringo," Marco said. "He's Thai."

"I don't care if he's Martian—has he checked out?"

"No," Marco said.

"Well he's got a Do Not Disturb sign on his door," Alma said.

"So? Knock. It's one o'clock," said Marco.

"I've knocked several times," Alma replied.

"So go in," Marco said.

"Remember what happened last week with that fat gringo?"

"He wasn't a gringo—he was German," Marco said.

Alma glared at him. Marco was being a prick.

"Would you call his room?" she asked.

"No," Marco said, turning away. "Just use your pass key and go in."

So Alma went back upstairs, gave Mr. Bunyasarn's door another loud knock, waited, sighed, took out her pass key, took a deep breath, and unlocked the door.

"Housekeeping," she said in English as she entered the room. It was one of the few English words she knew—that and the phrase "ask front desk." She repeated "Housekeeping" again as she stepped into the room.

The room was dark. The curtains were drawn tight. Alma reached over to the light switch and turned it on. She looked over to the bed. She could see Mr. Bunyasarn's body under the covers, neatly tucked in under a sheet and a light blanket. His head was resting on the pillow. He looked sound asleep.

"Señor?... Señor?... Housekeeping... Señor?" She kept repeating as she slowly walked up to the bed. Mr. Bunyasarn didn't move. His eyes were closed. His face was relaxed. He looked very peaceful.

Alma looked around. There was no one else in the room. There were no messes to clean up. The room looked very neat. The man's suitcase was sitting on the folding luggage stand in the corner. A briefcase and a small ice chest were on the floor next to the luggage stand. If she could get him up, Alma thought, she might be able to get the room cleaned up before the three o'clock check-in time. She reached down and pushed his shoulder. "Señor?" she said again.

She thought his shoulder didn't feel right. It moved but it was not normal to the touch... not warm enough. She looked again at his face.

"Señor?"

She didn't want to do it, but her hand reached out, as if by its own volition, and touched his face. It was cold. Her hand recoiled. She ran downstairs.

"Marco, Marco!" Alma blurted out at the front desk. "The gringo in room 323! I think he's dead!"

"Shhhhh," Marco said sternly. "Keep your voice down." He looked around. The lobby was almost empty—just a few gringos over in the corner having coffee. Nobody seemed to have heard Alma.

"Did you close the door?" he asked.

"What?"

"Did you close the door of the room when you left?"

"I...I...I don't know," Alma said.

"Well, go back and close it," Marco said coldly. He picked up the phone and started to dial.

"Are you calling the police?" Alma asked.

"Of course not, silly," Marco replied. "I'm calling Dr. Navarro. He'll do a death certificate, and he and his brother will take the body to the funeral home. Now go back and make sure the door is closed and locked. You can clean the room after Dr. Navarro and his brother remove the body."

Alma just stared at Marco, her mouth open. All she could say was, "I'm off at three-thirty."

"You're off when the room is cleaned. Now go make sure the door is closed."

*   *   *

Dr. Navarro had connections with all the hotels in the El Coco Barrio neighborhood in the town of La Chorrera.

Hotels, B&Bs, resorts, hostels—really any business that served tourists—needed someone like Dr. Navarro. People die all the time, but when someone dies in your business... well, it's just bad for business. Dr. Navarro appreciated that, and knew the monetary value of being discrete. Even though Panamanian law required the signature of three verifiable witnesses on a death certificate, a single doctor could sign if he personally knew the deceased...and Dr. Navarro always claimed he personally knew the deceased. Plus, his brother Pablo ran a local mortuary, so Dr. Navarro and Pablo could get any unfortunate deceased quickly and discreetly out of any business establishment and onto its final destination. It was a very satisfactory arrangement for all concerned. Pablo's mortuary needed bodies. Bodies needed doctors. The city needed death certificates. Hotels needed discretion. Everyone was happy. And, to be fair, most of Dr. Navarro's "patients" were elderly Panamanians, or undocumented freelance laborers in some unfortunate hotel remodeling accident, or occasionally some ill person, or more frequently, some victim of alcohol poisoning. As long as the body was not shot up, or cut up, or flattened... as long as Dr. Navarro could get away with claiming "natural causes"... he could sign the documents, get the body on a stretcher covered with a clean sheet, and out a side door, and into Pablo's waiting "ambulance." (Pablo's vehicle was painted to look like an ambulance, just to reassure any rubberneckers that the poor stricken patient might still pull through.)

In actuality, the majority of Dr. Navarro's cases were victims of guaro poisoning. Guaro was a homemade liquor brewed from sugar cane in backrooms and garages all over Latin America. It tasted sweeter than rum, cost only pennies to concoct, and one could easily add a little ethyl alcohol to the brew to give it a little extra kick, and sell it for a profit on the street corners to laborers and stupid tourists. But sometimes the kick was lethal, and that's when Dr. Navarro's diagnostic skills came in handy. He would jot down "cerebral hemorrhage" on the death certificate as Pablo wrapped the body, which, in a way, was not far from the mark. Guaro poisoning often caused brain bleeding.

However, if a body was riddled with bullets, had

multiple stab wounds, or was missing a head, he would do the right thing and call the police. Dr. Navarro was not without ethics, assuming that ethics was defined as "the risk that you might get in trouble if you mark an obvious murder victim as a natural-causes death."

And thus it unfolded with the lifeless body of Khambang Bunyasarn: Dr. Navarro and Pablo arrived quickly and quietly at the hotel, and spoke directly with Marco. Marco handed them a photocopy of Khambang's passport page. (Marco, of course, had made the copy of the photo page of Khambang's passport, as Panamanian law requires, when Khambang had checked in.) Marco escorted Dr. Navarro and Pablo upstairs and let them into Khambang's room and stood by and watched them (so they wouldn't steal anything) while they examined the body. Actually, Pablo examined the body while Dr. Navarro was busy filling out the death certificate.

Pablo first moved Khambang's head back and forth. The neck was stiff.

"I would say, Antonio, that rigor mortis is starting to fade, so I would put the time of death at maybe ten last night," Pablo said to his brother.

"Ten p.m." Dr. Navarro wrote down on the death certificate.

Pablo pulled the covers back to expose Khambang's naked chest. "The deceased is a well-nourished Asian male... What was his age, Antonio?"

Dr. Navarro looked at the passport and did some mental calculations. "Forty-five," he told Pablo.

"Yes," Pablo said, "a well-nourished Asian male of approximately forty-five. Cause of death appears to be a heart attack... Yes, definitely a heart attack, I would say... natural causes."

"Heart attack," Dr. Navarro wrote on the death certificate.

Pablo pulled the covers all the way off of Khambang and with one motion tossed them to the floor. Pablo was about to comment on how the deceased must have liked to sleep naked and how that surprised him because he thought Asians didn't do that. But those words never made it out of his mouth. Instead, Pablo ended up staring at the large pool of blood between Khambang's legs.

"Ahhh hmmm, Antonio, we have a problem here," Pablo said.

Dr. Navarro was checking the box marked "natural causes" and not looking at Pablo. "Yes," he said, "what is it?"

"You'd better look," Pablo said.

"Oh, okay," sighed Dr. Navarro, and put the death certificate down on the table and took off his reading glasses. He walked over to the bed.

"What exactly is...?" He stopped mid-sentence and stared at the blood. Then he muttered, "That's a lot of blood."

"Yes, I know," Pablo said.

Marco, who had all the while been standing in the corner, trying very hard not to look at the dead body, now was forced to look. Despite his reputation among the hotel staff for being a cold-hearted manager, Marco was actually very squeamish. Dead bodies made him nauseous. But when he heard Dr. Navarro say, "That's a lot of blood," he had to look. From where he was standing, he could clearly see the naked body of Khambang Bunyasarn, a short, pudgy and very naked middle-aged Asian man. He was completely devoid of body hair, except for the hair on the top of his head. There was not even a tiny tuft of hair around his wrinkled penis and scrotum. The thought flashed through Marco's mind how odd it was that a man's penis, the staff of his sexuality, the essence of his manhood, could look so deflated, useless and tiny in death. Equally quick was the microburst of thought in Marco's mind that the hotel was going to have to buy a new mattress. The weight and position of Khambang Bunyasarn's two legs had kept the blood from spreading out on the mattress. Instead, it formed a deep fjord of almost-black red that shimmered from underneath his scrotum all the way down to his knees. The edges had dried and seeped into the mattress, but the center had coagulated and glistened like a black glacier, a thick coating covering what Marco could only assume was a large amount of blood already soaking down into the mattress, maybe even into the box springs. He felt sick looking at it.

Pablo picked up the top sheet and light blanket that he had tossed off the bed and examined them. There was no blood. They must have been draped over the body's legs in such a way that they simply hadn't touched the blood. He dropped them back onto the floor.

"Could his appendix have ruptured?" Pablo asked his brother.

"No... well, no. He would have been in so much pain... for days... he would have told the hotel staff..." Dr. Navarro said, and then looked at Marco.

Marco just shook his head no. Khambang Bunyasarn hadn't said anything to anyone, and in fact he had looked fine the last time Marco saw him.

"Hemorrhoids?" suggested Pablo.

Dr. Navarro glanced at Pablo scornfully and just said, "Too much blood."

"Maybe he was a hemophiliac," Pablo said.

Dr. Navarro went to his black bag and took out a pair of latex gloves and put them on.

"Maybe he was a hemophiliac who got hemorrhoids... that could be natural causes..." Pablo suggested hopefully.

"Shut up and help me roll the body over," Dr. Navarro said.

Dr. Navarro pushed from his side of the bed and Pablo pulled from his side, and they rolled the body onto its side. Marco went for the easy chair in the corner of the room and sat down. He pulled the wastebasket close to him, just in case.

Dr. Navarro looked at Khambang's flabby ass. The blood had definitely come out of the man's anus. Dr. Navarro spread the small cheeks with his gloved hand and felt around in between the fleshy cheeks. He felt something odd. It felt like cloth. He gave it a gentle pull. It seemed to move. He bent down and held both ass cheeks apart and looked directly at the dead man's anus. There was a blood-soaked cloth stuff up the man's rectum.

"Okay Pablo," Dr. Navarro said. "Let's roll the body back." Pablo eased the body back over where it had previously lain.

"I'm afraid that you will have to call the police," Dr. Navarro said, looking at Marco. "There is a cloth, maybe a washcloth or something similar, stuffed up into man's rectum, obviously to stem the blood flow, although obviously it didn't work."

"Maybe he stuffed it up there himself," Pablo offered hopefully.

"In the realm of infinite possibilities, that is a possibility," Dr. Navarro said dryly as he removed his latex gloves. "But it would seem unlikely that he would be bleeding that profusely and then just lie down so peacefully to sleep. But in any case, I cannot say this man died of natural causes. He will need an autopsy, and *that*, as you know, Señor Marco, is outside of the services I offer."

Dr Navarro clicked his medical bag shut and said to Pablo, "Leave everything exactly the way it is now, Pablo. We need to leave and let Señor Marco attend to his obligations." Then he addressed Marco. "You should tell the police that you found the man unresponsive and so, of course, you immediately called a doctor, and that I arrived immediately and informed you the man was dead, and that you then, of course, called the police, all according to law and to the hotel's policies. No need to mention that Pablo was here. If the police want to talk to me, you have my number to give them. Come Pablo, let's go."

And with that, Dr. Navarro and Pablo left the room. Marco followed them out, locking the door behind him. He needed to move the guest who was scheduled to check into that room at three to another room, and then he would call the police.

Alma Vasquez was waiting for Marco in the lobby. Marco paused when he saw her. Did he need to tell her what to say to the police, he wondered to himself. No, he decided, there was no need to involve her at all.

"You can go home now, Alma," he said flatly to her. "I'll have someone else clean the room."

Chapter 2

There was a young man from Thailand,
who came to Panama with a grand plan...

La Chorrera was not a big Panamanian town, but it was growing, in large part because of the booming tourist business in nearby Panama City. Located only 25 miles southwest of Panama's capital, La Chorrera was developing a reputation as an expat-friendly town with affordable housing that still had a slightly wild side. It was a perfect base for the older tourist or expat who wanted to be close to the party scene of Panama City but have a quiet place to sleep off life's excesses.

And for those who didn't want to travel all the way to Panama City for their diversions, La Chorrera had a lot to offer. There were casinos, brothels, bathhouses, and massage parlors—nothing gaudy or flamboyant, mind you—and that was the exactly the charm of La Chorrera: understated excess, discrete sin, proper appearances.

The police chief of La Chorrera was Jorge Manuel, a rather young man to be a police chief. But Jorge Manuel's skill was in knowing exactly where his limitations were. While he had a certain even-handed management style that the rank and file police officers appreciated, Jorge Manuel also had the wisdom—uncharacteristic of youth—to know that he wasn't particularly skilled, that he wasn't well-trained in forensics, that he hadn't had a lot of experience as a police officer, much less a police chief, and that he owed his job to the influence of his uncle, don Fernando, who was the long-time police chief of the nearby town of Villa Rosario.

Don Fernando had been the police chief in Villa Rosario for over 30 years. He had a reputation for, shall we say, "expedient" law enforcement, and his political clout extended far beyond the tiny town of Villa Rosario. So when he wanted his nephew to be chosen as the police chief in La Chorrera, the mayor and the city fathers agreed, even if Jorge Manuel was not the most experienced person for the job.

But Jorge Manuel was learning. He brought in training seminars on police procedures from Panama City's Ministry of Public Security for all his officers to attend, and Jorge Manuel attended every one of those seminars alongside his officers. He encouraged his officers to ask questions, and he wasn't afraid to bring in experts from other cities to help on cases.

So it wasn't unusual for Jorge Manuel to tag along with the regular officers when some unusual case occurred. He usually stayed in the background, watching the more experienced officers do their job, learning what he could from them, and being a resource if they needed one. And thus, when he heard that there had been an unusual death at the Hotel de Cero, he simply decided to show up at the scene to see for himself.

But the moment Jorge Manuel got to the hotel room where Khambang's body lay, he sensed there was something wrong, and he decided he needed to do more than just observe. The sergeant in charge briefed him on what he had learned, which was basically what the desk clerk Marco had told him—that when this guest hadn't checked out, Marco had gone up to the room and knocked. Hearing no answer, he used his pass key to enter the room. When the guest did not awaken to the sound of Marco's voice, Marco assumed that he was ill and took it upon himself to call a doctor. But that when a doctor arrived, Marco was informed that the man was deceased, and that Marco then immediately called the police. It all sounded plausible, and maybe that's what bothered Jorge Manuel—it was too smooth.

After listening to the sergeant, Jorge Manuel went over and looked at the body. There was just too much blood, he thought. He must have been shot... but where?

The police photographer had finished taking pictures of the body.

"What do we know about this man?" Jorge Manuel

asked the sergeant.

"Just that he checked in two days ago."

"Alone?"

"Yes."

"Did he have any visitors?"

"According to the desk clerk, no."

"Do we have any identification?"

The sergeant handed Jorge Manuel the photocopy of Khambang's passport page that Marco had given him. Jorge Manuel looked at it. The single photocopy page only revealed the deceased's name, date of birth, photograph, and the fact that he was from Thailand. The fact that he was from Thailand was unusual. Panama didn't get a lot of Thai tourists. But other than that, the photocopy didn't reveal much. Jorge Manuel handed the page back to the sergeant.

"Let's turn the body over," he said.

He and the sergeant rolled the body over. Jorge Manuel bent down and stared at the man's ass. He could see the two smears in the blood on the man's buttocks that Dr. Navarro's fingers had left when Dr. Navarro had spread the man's asscheeks.

"Well, we are not the first to look at this butt," Jorge Manuel said to the sergeant, pointing to Dr. Navarro's finger marks. The sergeant nodded.

"Gabriel," Jorge Manuel called over to the camera man. "Come over here and take photos of this."

Gabriel came around the bed and took photos of where Jorge Manuel was pointing.

Jorge Manuel called over to the forensic officer. "Andrés, do you have an extra pair of latex gloves?" Andrés reached into his satchel of equipment and pulled out a pair and handed them to Jorge Manuel. Jorge Manuel put them on and felt around the man's asscheeks trying to find a bullet hole. He found none, but he did encounter the same cloth that Dr. Navarro had found.

"What the hell?" he said. "Andrés, bring a flashlight and shine it here."

Andrés did so, and Jorge Manuel, the sergeant, Gabriel, and Andrés all stared at the blood-soaked cloth that was wedged up the man's rectum.

"Take photos," Jorge Manuel said to Gabriel as he held the man's two asscheeks apart.

"What do you think, Capitán?" the sergeant asked him.

Jorge Manuel didn't know what to think. He had never heard of anyone bleeding to death out of their ass before. It was a very strange death, plus the man was from Thailand. A very unusual death. But Jorge Manuel remembered the advice of his uncle don Fernando to always treat any strange death as a homicide until you can prove otherwise.

"I think we'd better treat this as a murder scene until we can figure out what the hell is going on," Jorge Manuel said. "Andrés, dust the place for fingerprints... and take the dead man's fingerprints, too. Sergeant, call Dr. Espinoza and tell him we are going to need an autopsy. When Andrés is finished dusting the room, you can move the body to the morgue... and where is this desk clerk?"

"He's downstairs, Capitán."

"Can we get him up here, please. I'd like to talk with him."

The sergeant sent an officer down to get Marco. While he waited, Jorge Manuel looked around the room. Everything seemed orderly, very orderly. A suitcase was on the folding luggage rack, and a briefcase and ice chest were on the floor next to the luggage rack.

"Does the room have a safe?" Jorge Manuel suddenly asked the sergeant.

"It's in the bathroom closet," the sergeant said, "but the door was open and it was empty."

"Hmmm. Odd, don't you think?" Jorge Manuel said to the sergeant.

"Sí, Capitán."

"Andrés, dust the safe for prints too.'

A few minutes later, while Jorge Manuel was still standing by the bed looking at the body, a policeman brought Marco up to the room. Once again Marco started to feel nauseous. He stood by the doorway and tried not to look at the body. Jorge Manuel noticed his discomfort and was sympathetic.

"What is your name, muchacho?" Jorge Manuel asked Marco.

"Marco...Marco Torres," Marco responded.

"Were you the first one to discover the body, Marco?" Jorge Manuel asked.

Marco thought of Alma but decided to stick to his story. "Uh, sí, señor...sí. I guess I was."

Something about Marco's hesitation bothered Jorge Manuel.

"Tell me exactly how that happened."

"Um, well, this guest was supposed to check out by noon today. When he didn't, I came up and knocked at his door. He had a Do Not Disturb sign on his door, but it was almost one o'clock. When I got no answer, I used my pass key and entered the room. He looked asleep but did not awaken when I called to him loudly. So I... well I thought he might be sick, so I called a doctor..."

"Uh huh," said Jorge Manuel. "He was supposed to check out at noon?"

"Sí, señor."

"And you were downstairs at the front desk?"

"Sí, señor."

"And how did you know he hadn't checked out?" Jorge Manuel asked and smiled.

"Well, because he hadn't paid his bill."

"So you decided to come up and check on him?"

"Sí, señor."

Jorge Manuel hadn't stayed in many hotels in his life, but he had stayed in enough to know that it was the housekeepers who always pestered guests to get out of their rooms so they could clean, often before the guests were ready to vacate the room.

"Come over here, muchacho," Jorge Manuel said to Marco.

Marco walked over to the bed, trying not to look at the body.

"That's a lot of blood, don't you agree?" Jorge Manuel asked.

Marco was very uncomfortable now. "Sí, señor."

"Is there a housekeeper assigned to this floor?"

"Sí, señor."

"Was she supposed to clean this room?"

"Of course, señor."

"Did *she* knock on the door?"

"I—I suppose so, señor," Marco said, suddenly feeling cornered.

"Did she tell you she knocked on the door?"

"She might have, señor, yes, probably she would have..."

"Uh huh," said Jorge Manuel. "Did she come into the room, muchacho?"

"I—I don't know, señor..."

"What is the housekeeper's name, muchacho?"

"Alma...Alma Vasquez."

"Is she here now?" Jorge Manuel asked.

"No señor, she's gone for the day."

Jorge Manuel looked Marco straight in the eyes and asked, "Well, muchacho, suppose I were to find her today and ask her if she came into this room... What would she say?"

Marco felt the air go out of him. He had only wanted to tell a simple story, just enough so that the police would get the body out of the hotel, so he could return to his easy front desk job. But now he had screwed up, and this police chief was going to try and blame him for something he didn't do.

"She...she would say that she told me that she had come into the room and could not rouse the guest."

"Ok, and did you come up here then?"

"No, señor, I called the doctor then."

"I see," said Jorge Manuel. "And what doctor did you call?"

"Uh...a Dr. Navarro," stammered Marco.

"Ah, Antonio Navarro?" asked Jorge Manuel.

"Sí, señor."

"Not exactly the first choice of doctors to treat a *sick* man, is he?" Jorge Manuel asked. "His reputation is more in treating dead men, wouldn't you say?"

Marco lowered his head and said nothing.

"You knew this man was dead when you called Dr. Navarro," Jorge Manuel said.

"Sí...I thought...I thought that was the case, señor."

"Because this Alma woman had told you that, right?"

"Sí, señor."

"Okay, muchacho, so you lied to the sergeant here about finding the body, and you tried to lie to me... but I might be willing to overlook that if you tell us the truth now. Understand?"

"Sí, señor."

"When did this man check in?"

"Two days ago," Marco replied.

"Was this his first time here?"

Jorge Manuel sensed Marco's hesitation, so he added, "Muchacho, you are on the edge of spending the night in jail. Better to tell us the truth."

"Sí, señor," Marco said. "It was not his first time here. He stays here frequently."

"Really?" Jorge Manuel asked. "How often has he been here?"

"This is maybe his fifth or sixth time this year."

"Really? And how long does he stay for?"

"Two nights... never more than two nights," Marco replied.

"So he's not a tourist," Jorge Manuel said, more to himself than to Marco.

"Well, señor, yes and no..." Marco replied.

"Explain," Jorge Manuel said.

Marco took a deep breath. "I think his first day is always business," Marco said. "He wears a suit. A few hours after he checks in, three men—also in suits—always show up, and they all go up to his room. They stay for about thirty minutes, and then they leave. But they come back, usually about an hour later, and this time they stay longer, maybe an hour. But they leave before dinner time. But the second night, the men come back in the evening, but they are not in suits, and they usually bring guests, and they stay a long time."

"These men are Panamanians?" Jorge Manuel asked.

"No señor, two are Asian, one is a gringo."

"Always the same three men?"

"Sí, señor."

"And these guests they bring on the second night, who are they?"

Marco looked down. He didn't want to get in trouble with the hotel, but he didn't want to get in trouble with this police chief either. "Well, they are women… you know, party girls."

Jorge Manuel rubbed his chin. This still didn't make much sense to him. "How do you know the first night was business?" he asked Marco.

"Well, he always brings that dry ice chest," said Marco, pointing to the small cooler in the corner next to Khambang's luggage. "He checks in with it, but when the three men leave the first time, they always take it away with them. But when they come back an hour or so later, they bring it back with them. And they are always very serious on the first day, but they always look ready to party on the second day. So I always assumed this man was bringing something to them."

"Hmmm," Jorge Manuel said, "maybe you should be a detective, no?" and smiled. Marco started to feel a bit better to see Jorge Manuel smile. Maybe he wouldn't get into trouble after all.

"And how do you know it is a *dry* ice chest, muchacho?"

"Because one time when the man checked in, he asked me where he could get dry ice, so I figured…I assumed it was for the ice chest."

Jorge Manuel nodded his head and thought for a minute. It sounded like a drug delivery, but he didn't understand about the ice chest. Did dry ice somehow disguise the odor of drugs from police dogs? It didn't make sense. He looked over at the ice chest. It was small but very conspicuous with a large red cross on the side.

"Did this man come into Panama at the airport?" he asked Marco.

"I don't know, señor."

"How did he arrive at the hotel?"

"By taxi."

"Okay, ok... oh, and you let Dr Navarro into the room, right?"

"Sí, señor."

"Was his brother with him?"

"Sí, señor."

"And you were here when Dr. Navarro examined the body?"

Sí, señor."

At this point the sergeant stepped over and whispered into Jorge Manuel's ear. Jorge Manuel nodded and then asked Marco, "Was the sheet and blanket on the floor when you came up to the room with Dr. Navarro?"

"No, señor. They were over the body."

"Were the sheets in disarray, tangled up?" Jorge Manuel asked.

"No, señor. Everything was neat. The man looked like he was sleeping."

"No blood on the sheet?"

"I did not see any," Marco responded.

"And Dr. Navarro took the sheet off the man and threw it to the floor?"

"His brother did."

"And then what happened?" Jorge Manuel asked.

"They saw the blood, and they rolled him over and looked at his backside."

"And what did they say?"

Marco shifted his weight and stammered, "Dr. Navarro said...he said there was a cloth stuck up the man's ass. That's when he told me I had to call the police."

"Okay, okay," said Jorge Manuel. "I think that's all the questions I have for now."

"Señor," Marco said, "can I ask a favor? We're not supposed to let the party girls up to the rooms, but I always did for this man, because, well, because he always tipped me well. Can you not tell the hotel management that I did that?"

"Who else knew about his parties?" Jorge Manuel asked.

"Just Tomás, the nighttime desk clerk. I shared some of the tip money with him so he would be quiet, too."

"I understand, muchacho. I can't promise it won't come out, but I don't need to tell anyone right now."

"Gracias, señor."

"Sergeant," Jorge Manuel said, "can you have one of your officers go with this muchacho back down to the front desk and get his address and phone number and also the names, addresses, and the phone numbers of the housekeeper and the nighttime desk clerk? Thank you."

After Marco left with one of the police officers, Jorge Manuel glanced over at Andrés, the forensic technician. Andrés was just finishing his fingerprint dusting, and Gabriel was taking pictures of the room.

"Are you finding much, Andrés?"

"No, Capitán, nothing yet."

"Well, take your time with this room, Andrés. I want you to be thorough. But when you are done dusting for prints—and don't forget the dead man's fingers too—I want you to bag up his suitcase, his briefcase, and especially that ice chest, and any other personal items you find in the room, and bring them to the station and carefully inventory them, and let me know what you find as soon as possible."

Jorge Manuel then turned to the sergeant and said, "Sergeant, thank you for permitting me to intrude on your good work here. I apologize for any delays I might have caused. I will leave you in peace now. Let's chat later at the station."

"Sí, Capitán, gracias."

As Jorge Manuel left the hotel, he thought to himself, "This is too weird. Too many things don't make sense: the amount of blood, the calm expression of the dead man, the cloth stuffed up his ass, the open safe... I only hope he was not someone important."

Chapter 3

There was a young man from Thailand
who came to Panama with a grand plan,
but things went awry,
and bullets did fly...

It was three days later that don Fernando got the phone call from Jorge Manuel.

After the traditional ten minutes of conversation about family and health, Jorge Manuel got to the reason for his call.

"Don Fernando, I am afraid I need your help. I have a case here, a very unusual case, a murder case, from three days ago."

"A murder? In La Chorrera? I did not read anything in the newspaper about this," don Fernando said.

"No, the newspapers don't know about it," Jorge Manuel replied.

"Ah, that's good. Was it a Panameño?" don Fernando asked.

"No, a turista,"

"Any witnesses?"

"No. He died in a hotel. A housekeeper found him."

"Is he someone important?"

"No, in fact, no one has made any inquiry. No one has filed a missing persons report. No one has even called the hotel looking for him, and as I said, this happened three days ago."

"Well, Koke," don Fernando laughed, addressing Jorge Manuel by his family nickname, "I don't see why you need me. This is just another unfortunate turista death, no? Some extranjero does something he shouldn't and dies. No one's making waves about it—so why make extra work?"

"This one has got some bad omens with it, uncle, some very bad omens. It's too complicated to explain by phone. I just got the lab reports today, and I was wondering, uncle, if I could meet with you and your friend Señor Landes, and show you the autopsy reports, the forensic reports, and get advice from both of you. It's a very bizarre case, and I think it involves a network of other people, some of them gringos."

Don Fernando paused. He had a lot of faith in his nephew's judgment. For Jorge Manuel to ask him to bring his American friend Dan Landes with him meant that he thought the case was big—bigger than even don Fernando could handle.

"Of course, Koke, I am always glad to help. I will call Dani and see when he is free and call you back... although, I must warn you, he is a different man than when you last saw him."

"It's only been—what?—a year?" Jorge Manuel asked.

"Many things can happen in a year, Koke. He went to the states and came back... well... different. His mind is still good, though. It's just that, he's a little strange now. You'll see how it is. But let me see if he's in town. Maybe we could come to La Chorrera tomorrow afternoon.

"Yes, uncle. Please."

*   *   *

The fact was, Jorge Manuel knew very little about Dan Landes. He knew that Dan was an expat, a retired detective from Los Angeles, and that he had been don Fernando's friend in Panama for the last ten years or so, but that was about it. Don Fernando always kept his own personal life, and the lives of his friends, very private, even to his nephew. But don Fernando had introduced Dan Landes to his nephew about a year ago, when don Fernando had brought Dan along to help Jorge Manuel on murder case in a local bathhouse in La Chorrera, and Jorge Manuel had been very impressed with Dan's detective skills. And it was true that Dan had helped solve that case very quickly, but only Dan knew that it had largely been a matter of pure luck. Dan's experience and training back in L.A. had only been in white-collar crime, not homicide, but Jorge Manuel didn't know that. Besides, even if he had known that, Jorge Manuel felt he needed all the expert help he could get with this Khambang Bunyasarn case.

*　*　*

Dan Landes was lying in his bed thinking about rings when don Fernando telephoned him. The rings he was thinking about were of different colors, and they seemed to be floating in space, like the rings of Saturn, right in front of his eyes, even though Dan was aware that they were actually just thoughts and not real rings.

He took another small sip of ayahuasca from the plastic bottle by his bed and thought to himself: "What if I moved my eyes left, would that change the color or the spinning of the rings?" He tried it, moving his gaze quickly to the left. The rings stayed in place, spinning slowly, but the eye movement made Dan feel dizzy.

"That's odd," he thought. "Why would it make me feel dizzy? Could I make someone else feel dizzy if I moved my eyes to the right?"

Just then the phone rang. The colored rings of Saturn evaporated in space like smoke. Dan reached over to the phone.

"Ah Dani, you are home," don Fernando said when Dan answered.

"Of course, don Fernando, where else would I be?" Dan answered cheerfully.

"Well, I was worried you might be up in the mountains, you know... hiking."

"Hmmm, yeah... well, I'm here today. What's up?"

"I need a favor. You remember Jorge Manuel, the police chief in La Chorrera?"

"Yes... how could I forget," Dan said bitterly. "Why do you ask?"

"Well, he needs some advice. Can I talk you into coming with me to La Chorrera tomorrow to meet with

29

him? There has been this unfortunate death there of some tourist—"

But Dan interrupted him. "Yeah, no thanks, don Fernando, not a fucking chance. The last time I went with you to help out your little friend, I had to witness someone being fucking killed right in front of me."

"Oh, Dani," don Fernando laughed, "are you still obsessed about that? We have talked and talked about that case. It was unfortunate, but as you gringos say, sometimes shit happens."

Dan took a deep breath. "No... no, I've gotten over that case," he admitted, "but I don't want to repeat it. I don't want to see any more dead bodies."

"Well then, mi amigo, this case will be perfect for you. This guy died days ago. This favor I ask is only about paperwork, just paper. We go to La Chorrera tomorrow, have coffee with Jorge Manuel, maybe eat some sweet pastries, and you read through his reports and give him your opinion."

"What kind of reports?" Dan asked.

"An autopsy, some lab reports, that's all," don Fernando said.

"He doesn't need me for that... What are you not telling me?" Dan asked.

Don Fernando laughed. "I am only not telling you what I don't know, Dani. Some turista died in a hotel three days ago. They did an autopsy. No one's claimed the body. It's not even in the papers. Jorge Manuel thinks it's a murder, but I don't know why. He only asked that you and I read the reports he has and give him our opinions. An hour of your time, nothing more."

"Why does he need me for that?" Dan repeated.

Don Fernando sighed. "Ah Dani, I do not know, believe me, I do not know. What I've told you is all he told me. He thinks he has some huge problem, but I don't know what it is. Do me a favor, Dani, and come with me tomorrow."

"Oh fuck... okay, don Fernando. Just to read reports. Okay, I'll tag along. But that's all, entiende? Nothing more."

"Ah Dani, eres un amigo verdadero. I will pick you up at 12:30. Maybe we can get Jorge Manuel to spring for lunch.

I'll tell him to take us to that nice restaurant Los Cuñados. I like the food there. See you tomorrow."

Don Fernando hung up the phone and said a silent "whew" to himself. He had been worried that Dan was going to turn him down... and he understood why. Dan's synopsis of last year's events was accurate. Don Fernando had taken Dan to La Chorrera to help Jorge Manuel with an investigation of a murder in a gay bathhouse, and Dan did end up witnessing the murder suspect being shot and killed right in front of him. Don Fernando had not anticipated the impact that this was going to have on his friend. He had assumed that Dan had seen lots of people being killed back in L.A., but he later learned that wasn't true. Plus, this had been a particularly violent killing. Dan had been standing about fifteen feet away when the suspect's head was blown half off by a bullet. In the weeks afterwards, don Fernando was worried that Dan was going to have a nervous breakdown. When Dan told him that he was going back to the states to "figure things out," don Fernando assumed he would never see his friend again. But after almost a year, Dan came back to Panama and moved back into his old apartment, and things had been good, relatively speaking, since then. They had resumed their friendship and Dan seemed to have gotten over whatever emotional trauma he had been going through. The only fly in the ointment was that once every two or three months, Dan would go up into the Panama mountains for a week at a time to collect ayahuasca leaves and brew and drink the traditional indigenous liquor. He and Dan only discussed it one time, and don Fernando's sense was that it was a topic best avoided. But other than this one sensitive area, don Fernando was glad to have his old friend back.

*　*　*

The next day, don Fernando drove Dan to El Restaurante de Los Cuñados in La Chorrera. Miguel, one of the owners of the restaurant, greeted don Fernando and Dan at the door and walked them to a private table in a back room where Jorge Manuel was waiting. Don Fernando had met Miguel before, but did not know him well. He did notice that Miguel greeted Dan.

"Do you know him?" don Fernando whispered to Dan as they walked back to the private room.

"He's a friend of Ricardo's," Dan whispered back.

"Oh, I see," don Fernando said, and stored that information away in his brain. Don Fernando of course knew Ricardo, the old gringo writer who lived alone in Villa Rosario, and he knew Ricardo was gay, so he wondered if this Miguel fellow was also gay, but then he remembered that Miguel had a wife. So it must simply be, don Fernando concluded, that Ricardo liked this restaurant too—he probably came here often to eat, and got to know Miguel because he was a frequent customer.

Jorge Manuel stood up when don Fernando and Dan entered the room and embraced both of them.

"Thank you so much for taking the time to come all the way here," Jorge Manuel said. "I know both of you are very busy and I appreciate it."

Dan just smiled and nodded. In fact, he was never busy. This was the first time he had left his apartment in several days.

Miguel re-entered the room and brought a pitcher of water for the table. Then he returned with menus. Don Fernando and Jorge Manuel chatted together. Dan took the menu that Miguel handed him and perused it. Ricardo had always said that this was his favorite restaurant in La Chorrera, but Dan had never eaten here before. But the choices looked good. He wasn't all that hungry. But he figured that he might as well order something because, despite don Fernando assuring him that this meeting would only take an hour, Dan knew it would be more like three hours.

And Dan was correct. Miguel came back to take their lunch orders, and Jorge Manuel got down to business, starting with the case background. He shared what Marco had told him about how Khambang Bunyasarn's would come to the hotel approximately once a month and always stay for two nights; about how the same three men—two Asians and a gringo—would visit him on the first day in what looked like some official capacity; about how they would take the ice chest when they left the first day but always return it within an hour or so; about how the three men would then return on the evening of the second day in a more jovial mood and bring prostitutes with them, and stay late into the evening. He described the room at the Hotel de Cero where Khambang's body was found; he described the amount of blood in the bed; he passed around photographs of the body; he described the bloody cloth that was wedged up Khambang's ass; and then he got to what the autopsy had revealed, and what explained all the blood that was on the bed: four bullets inside the body.

"Here's the x-ray of the man's chest," Jorge Manuel said, holding up a large print. "You can see one bullet lodged in the left lung, two bullets that tore through the heart and stopped in the sternum; and one just to the right of the heart below this rib."

Don Fernando looked confused. "How did they get inside the man?" he asked.

Dan spoke up for the first time. "It's an old Viet Cong trick," he said flatly, "and the killer was an amateur."

Both don Fernando and Jorge Manuel were startled by Dan's tone of voice and stared at him.

"What is a 'Viet Cong'?" Jorge Manuel finally asked.

Dan looked at him and started to frown, but then realized how young Jorge Manuel actually was. "Well, you would call them terrorists nowadays," Dan said. "Back during the Vietnam War, starting in the mid-nineteen-fifties, the Viet Cong was a political group—a political group *and* an army— that operated in South Vietnam but worked for the North Vietnam communists. Anyway, one of the ways they would kill American soldiers was that the Viet Cong women would go to bars and let themselves be picked up by Americans, go to some hotel, but then they would spike the soldier's drink, so the soldier would pass out, then they would stick a gun up their ass and shoot them. The fact that the muzzle of the gun was jammed so far up the soldier's rectum would act like a silencer, so no one would hear the gunshot. Sometimes they would hold a pillow over the soldier's torso as extra soundproofing. It was a good job for women because they didn't need a high-caliber gun. A small pistol would do the trick. I bet the bullets you pulled out of this body," Dan pointed at the x-ray, "were small caliber." Jorge Manuel nodded yes. Dan continued, "The other reason you want a small pistol is that you want the bullets to stay inside the body. You don't want a gun with a lot of power. But the reason I say this shooter was an amateur is that normally you'd just need one shot. As long as you hit the heart, the man was dead or going to be dead very soon. This shooter used four bullets. That's why there was so much blood. And that's why he—or she—had to use a cloth to jam up the man's ass—to try and stop the bleeding. When the Viet Cong first started using this assassination method, a lot of deaths weren't even classified as murders. Because there was no blood, no bullet wounds, there wasn't an autopsy, and the Army thought the soldiers just drank themselves to death or overdosed on heroin. But eventually the Army figured it out. Dan paused, and looked at the x-ray again. "But this guy… and for some reason I think the shooter was a guy, not a woman… this guy was an amateur. It's just sloppy shooting." He looked up at Jorge Manuel. "How much drugs were in this guy's system?"

"Well, I was going to ask you about that," Jorge Manuel said, pulling a report from a manila folder. "There were a lot of drugs, but I've never heard of these names before… xylazine, gamma-hydroxybutyrate , methaqualone—well, I've heard of that one—and rohypnol… plus, of course, alcohol."

"Jesus," Dan said. "More proof that these guys were amateurs. They didn't need all of those. Um, let me see the report." Dan looked at it quickly. "Well, xylazine is a horse tranquilizer; rohypnol is what we call in the states a 'date rape' drug—it knocks you out. Gamma-hydroxybutyrate is GHB, another date rape drug; and methaqualone, well that's Quaalude, as you know… interesting… They really wanted this guy unconscious… And if they put all this into one drink, he'd be zonked out in under a minute, maybe 30 seconds, maybe less...." Dan thought for a moment, then said out loud, "So he was drugged, stripped of his clothes and laid out in the bed—or maybe he was already naked in the bed when he passed out—and someone put a gun up his ass and shot him." Dan looked at Jorge Manuel and explained, "The idea is to make it look like a natural death; but they fucked it up, so they tried to cover it up and got out of there as fast as they could.... Anyone see who was with this guy the night he was shot?"

"The nighttime desk clerk said three men came to his hotel room with some girls," Jorge Manuel said. "As far as we can tell, these were the same three men who met with the victim every time he came to Panama."

"Ah," Dan said. "Now we're getting somewhere." He closed his eyes and tried to visualize the hotel lobby. "Tell me exactly what the night clerk saw the night before the body was found," he said to Jorge Manuel.

"Well the three men came back to the hotel that night, and they brought two prostitutes with them," Jorge Manuel explained. "The night clerk recognized the girls— they are local prostitutes, but expensive ones, you know, escort girls.... Anyway, they came back with the girls, and as usual, they had a grocery bag with bottles of liquor, and they went up to the room, just like normal. The hotel doesn't really allow that type of activity. But the victim, well, he would slip the day-time manager some money, and the day-time manager gave some of it to the night clerk, so they both turned a blind eye to the prostitutes. Besides, this group was never noisy. They never disturbed the other guests. So everything was normal—like it always was—except, *usually* the three men would leave the hotel after midnight and one or more of the girls would stay in the room until the morning. But this time, about an hour or two after everyone arrived, one of the men escorted the two girls out. That had never happened before—the girls leaving early like that— but the night clerk didn't think anything about it. Maybe the victim didn't like these girls, who knows? I mean, both the day-time manager and the night clerk always assumed that the three men were bringing the girls up to the room for the entertainment of the guest, Mr. Bunyasarn. So the night clerk just assumed that either Mr. Bunyasarn didn't like the girls or didn't feel like having sex with them. At any rate, the man took the girls away, and then he returned, and then about thirty minutes later, all three men left."

Dan opened his eyes and said, "Okay, here's what happened: The three men planned to kill this guy. They bring the girls up as normal, and they all have some drinks and relax, but then when this Khambang guy gets a little tipsy, they spike his drink. When he passes out, they make excuses to the girls, but still pay them full price, and one guy escorts them out while the other men clean the room, wiping away any fingerprints. When the one guy returns, they shoot the victim, but they fuck it up, and so they stuff something up his ass, and scramble out of there… I assume you didn't find any fingerprints."

Jorge Manuel just stared at Dan. How did this gringo figure stuff out so fast? How was he so sure? Jorge Manuel looked over at don Fernando, who was just sitting there peacefully watching his friend work.

"No, señor, you are correct. Everything was wiped clean. No prints anywhere," Jorge Manuel said.

"Well," Dan said, "then all you have to work with is trying to get good descriptions of these three men from the witnesses… Did they use the same prostitutes each time?"

"Usually, señor, but not always."

"Well, still, if I were you, I would try and locate these last two hookers, and any other hookers that the three guys hired in the past few months. Maybe one of them said something to one of the hookers that will lead you to where these three guys are staying or where they usually stay when they're in town."

Jorge Manuel nodded his head. Dan's suggestion made sense.

Dan continued speaking, "But other than that, I don't have any other suggestions. I mean, it's really a simple case, even though it's a bizarre way to kill someone. But basically… what you have is a dead body, with no direct eye-witnesses to the murder, but with three persons of interest and some more people to interview."

But then Jorge Manuel said, "Sí, Señor Landes, but we have this other piece of evidence that complicates this case..."

"Yeah? What's that?" Dan asked.

"It's the ice chest. We took it to the police lab in Panama City—as you know, we don't have a good forensic lab in our little town—but we originally thought this Asian might be a drug smuggler—that he was smuggling drugs into the country in the ice chest to deliver to the three men. That made sense to us, except for the dry ice..."

"What dry ice?" Dan asked.

"Well, we think, Señor Landes, that whatever Mr. Bunyasarn was carrying in the ice chest was packed in dry ice, because one time he asked the desk clerk where he could buy dry ice—but we don't know why he needed dry ice. Nonetheless, we originally assumed it was drugs. Our original theory was that he brought the drugs into the country, but for some reason the three men needed to test the drugs each time... so the first meeting was formal and short. Mr. Bunyasarn would hand over the ice chest and the men would leave. A short time later, the men would return the ice chest. We originally assumed they had removed the drugs for testing, and then if the tests showed the drugs were of good quality, the men would return the second day to pay Mr. Bunyasarn and they would all celebrate with some prostitutes... This was our original theory, because it fit the facts."

"You keep saying 'original theory'... but evidently that is no longer your theory," Dan said.

"That is correct, Señor Landes. We took the ice chest to the lab thinking they might find traces of some drug and maybe explain why the dry ice was necessary... and they found something, but it wasn't drugs."

Dan gave Jorge Manuel a quick cold look. "What did they find?"

"They didn't know what it was at first... it was tissue, like muscle, just a small bloody smear on the inside walls of the ice chest, so we changed our theory and thought that Mr.

Bunyasarn was smuggling human organs... you know... for transplant. That would explain the dry ice and help account for so many Asians involved. It's a big business in Asia, you know... but the lab analyzed the tissue, and it wasn't human... or rather, it was part human..."

"What do you mean?" don Fernando suddenly asked.

"We don't know yet," Jorge Manuel said. "The lab only could say that this muscle tissue was animal—that it contained some human cells—but they were mixed with some pig cells that didn't belong. They had never seen anything like it. It was, they said, half-human, half-pig."

The table fell quiet. Don Fernando looked confused. Dan was deep in thought. Jorge Manuel felt suddenly exhausted. He was hoping that somehow in telling the story to his uncle and to Dan Landes, that somehow it would make sense. But it still baffled him.

Finally Dan spoke. "Well, that doesn't change anything... at least not yet... You still simply have a murder victim and three persons of interest and some people to interview... Whatever the tissue was, well... it may have *motivated* the murder but that just means it's just a motive. Doesn't matter if it was drugs, gold, human organs, or something else. It doesn't alter the investigative procedure. You still need to track down those hookers, maybe see if you can get some artist sketches of these three men, and find out more about this Bunyasarn fellow... Have you contacted the Thai embassy yet?"

"No, Señor Landes, we just got these reports yesterday. I was waiting to talk with you two."

"Well, I would contact the embassy... maybe let the newspaper know... well, I would only let the paper know there was a death—I wouldn't call it a murder. If these three guys are still in town, you don't want to spook them. Just say someone passed away—just to get this guy's name into the paper in case anyone else knows him. With the embassy I would be more candid, but tell them to keep it quiet. But see if you can find out who this guy is... or *was*... and what his background was... As for the ice chest... well, there's an FBI lab in the states, in Bethesda, Maryland, that does DNA analysis for a lot of state police departments. You might inquire and see if you can send the ice chest there for analysis... It would be interesting to know what this tissue actually is, but I don't see how it changes any of the work you have to do."

Dan Landes' words made sense to Jorge Manuel. He admired the gringo's ability to prioritize things and not get overwhelmed. Still, the ice chest bothered him.... How can flesh be part-human?

Dan gave Jorge Manuel a quick glance and smiled. "You are bothered by the ice chest?" Dan asked.

Jorge Manuel was surprised. Were his feelings that transparent? He nodded his head yes. "Sí, Señor Landes, it does not seem natural to me... that something could be part-human. It goes against God's plan."

"Ahhh," said Dan, "I see... well mi amigo, there are many things in today's medicine that are part-human... for example, we put pig valves in human hearts to save lives, don't we? We don't say the man is part-pig, do we? And yet...." Dan smiled at Jorge Manuel, and added, "I am sure there is a simple explanation for the ice chest."

At that moment, Miguel entered the room with a large tray. He placed plates of food in front of each man. Each of the three men ate in silence. Don Fernando was pleased that his friend could advise his nephew; Jorge Manuel was thinking that a man with a pig valve in his chest really was part-pig; and Dan was pondering whether there was some Thai criminal enterprise trafficking human organs through Panama.

Chapter 4

There was a young man from Thailand
who came to Panama with a grand plan,
but things went awry,
and bullets did fly,
and now he's in forever goodbyeland

Dan woke up the next afternoon. Since returning to Panama several months ago, his sleeping pattern had been all over the map. Sometimes he'd wake up at the crack of dawn; other times he'd sleep until mid-afternoon. He didn't mind the irregular hours, but he always had to think for a minute when he did wake up: What day is this? What time is it? How long had he been sleep?

He reached down to the floor of his bed and grabbed the plastic bottle and looked at the remaining contents—less than a eighth of a bottle left. Soon he would have to make a trip up into the mountains. Maybe tomorrow. He brought the bottle to his lips and took a tiny sip and let the smoky pungent liquid slide down his throat. He placed the bottle back on the floor, then lay back in bed. He held his hands up to his face and looked at them for a minute. Then he fluffed up his pillow, closed his eyes and relaxed.

For some reason, he started wondering about this Khambang fellow. He didn't give a damn about the case, yet somehow he was curious if Jorge Manuel was having any luck finding out who this guy was. Maybe he wasn't a criminal. Maybe he was just a businessman who got robbed and murdered. But robbed of what? And why was his hotel room wiped clean of any prints? That implied the murder was premeditated.

Dan started recalling the photos that Jorge Manuel had shown him of the hotel room and the body. He let the image of each photo hover in space, and then let them expand so he could examine every detail of each photo. Here was the bed... here was the blood trapped in the bed by the man's two legs... here was the security safe in the bathroom closet, the door wide open, empty of any contents... here was the ice chest with the big red cross on the side... here were the photos of the fingerprint dust on the furniture—lots of dust, but no prints....

In his mind's eye, Dan put himself in Khambang's hotel room. He just stood there in the corner and watched how the big gringo was explaining to the two prostitutes that their friend had had too much to drink. The two Thai men were helping Khambang over to the bed. Khambang was still conscious, but starting to nod out. He couldn't stand on his own. The two Thai men eased him into the bed. By the time his head hit the pillow, he was out. The gringo was saying to the two girls that this was their lucky night because they would still receive full payment but didn't have to do any work. Dan looked at the gringo. He was a big man, on the thick side, older, clean-shaven. The gringo was speaking Spanish to the two hookers, but his Spanish had an accent... German? Russian? Dan looked at this face and realized he wasn't from North America, but from somewhere Slavic, some Eastern European country... Dan decided he was Bulgarian. The Bulgarian started counting out money to the women. The two hookers were smiling—this *was* their lucky night, they thought. He paid them and told them that the other man would take them home. One of the two Thai men smiled and walked over to the girls. The two girls stood up, and he left with them.

The Bulgarian's face changed as soon as the first Thai was out the door with the two girls.

"Come on," he said to the remaining Thai, "we don't have much time."

They stripped Khambang of his clothes, folded the clothes neatly, and placed them in the suitcase. Khambang was now lying naked on the bed, completely and deeply unconscious.

"Let me show you how this is done," the Bulgarian was saying to the Thai. The Bulgarian pulled a pistol from a shoulder holster. Dan looked at it. It was a long-barreled Ruger .22 caliber. The Bulgarian was saying to the Thai, "The trick is you need a long barrel, at least five inches long, and nothing stronger than a .22 caliber. Now watch and learn."

The Bulgarian pulled a small tube out of his pocket, uncapped it, and squeezed a clear lubricant up and down the barrel of the pistol. Dan guessed it was a tube of K-Y jelly.

"It's not necessary to do this," the Bulgarian explained to the Thai, but it makes it easier."

When he finished, he recapped the tube and put it back in his pocket. Then he rolled Khambang's naked body over on one side. Khambang's arm flopped over. The Bulgarian pulled one asscheek aside and shoved the barrel of the pistol as far up into Khambang's ass as he could. The Thai came around to that side of the bed to watch.

"You have to get the barrel way up there, you see? And aim straight up into the body," and with that, the Bulgarian pulled the trigger. There was a little pop, like popcorn, and Khambang's body jerked hard.

"Now, you try it," the Bulgarian said, and stepped aside, leaving the black handle of the gun sticking absurdly out of the naked buttocks.

The Thai stepped up and grabbed the gun's handle and pulled the trigger. Again, there was a little pop. Again, Khambang's body jerked.

"No, that was too far left," the Bulgarian said, "You want to aim right in the middle. Try again."

The Thai man hunched over a bit, looking at Khambang's upper torso, and pulled the trigger again. There was another pop, but this time Khambang's body didn't jerk.

"Ah, too far right. Aim for the middle," the Bulgarian said gruffly.

The Thai bent over again, took aim, and pulled the trigger once more. Pop.

"That was better," the Bulgarian said. "That's enough. Let's lay him flat." The Bulgarian pulled the gun out of Khambang's ass, and let the dead body flop over on its back. He reached into one of the grocery bags and got a cloth rag and wiped the lubricant off the gun barrel, inspecting it carefully, and then returned the gun to his shoulder holster. Then the two men stretched Khambang out on the bed so that his body was straight, and folded his arms peacefully over his chest.

"Okay, let's wipe this place down," the Bulgarian said, and the two men grabbed cloth rags from the grocery bags and started wiping all the light switches, tables tops, chair arm rests, and door handles. They placed the suitcase on the luggage stand and the briefcase and ice chest on the floor next to the luggage stand, and wiped them all clean of prints. The Bulgarian went into the bathroom and came back a minute later, stuffing a bundle of cash into his pocket. "Got the money," he said. "Bathroom's clean."

The two men continued cleaning until the first Thai man returned to the room from escorting the hookers home. "We're almost done," the Bulgarian said to him.

"You know, Krasko, this man is bleeding," the first Thai said to the Bulgarian.

"What?" The Bulgarian came over and looked at the pool of blood that was starting to form between Khambang's upper thighs.

"Shit!" the Bulgarian said. "We used too many bullets. Shit!"

The Bulgarian took the cloth he had been cleaning with, and with one sweep of his large left arm, scooped up Khambang's legs just under the knee, lifted them high, and stuffed the cleaning cloth into the asshole that was oozing blood. The Bulgarian jammed the cloth in with his thumb and then lowered Khambang's legs, and repositioned them on the bed.

"Damn it to hell," the Bulgarian said. "Puii," he said to the second Thai, "grab the sheet and blanket over there. Help me spread them out over the body. Yes, that's it. Now pull tight so they don't touch the blood and tuck your side in."

The two men tucked in the sheet and blanket so the top was tight over the dead Khambang.

"Let's get out of here," the Bulgarian said. "I'll wipe the door."

Dan watched as all three men exited the room, with

the Bulgarian going last, wiping the door and doorknobs as he left.

Dan looked over at Khambang. A blue circle, like one of Saturn's rings, was spinning over the body. "Cold as outer space," Dan thought to himself.

The scene faded, and Dan was standing in a muddy field next to a wooden pen full of pigs. There was a farmer leaning against the pen, chewing on tobacco and talking to a man whose face Dan couldn't see.

"These are special pigs," the farmer was saying, "We grow them for their heart valves. Best heart valves in the country. When it's harvest time, we have to butcher them real fast, and then pack the hearts in dry ice. That fancy medical company comes to my farm in a helicopter to pick them up. In a helicopter! Can you believe that? Why, we make more money on one pig heart than my daddy did on a whole herd of bacon—it's unbelievable. After we harvest the hearts, I sell the rest of the pig to Lonnie down the road. He preps them and sells the meat to that barbecue joint over in Bristow. Damn rednecks come from miles around to eat that BBQ... ha! Good thing they don't know about all the antibiotics and chemicals I gotta feed these pigs to grow them hearts so big. Hooha."

That image faded and Dan was back in his bed, coming out of his reverie. He looked at his hands. They seemed normal. "What an odd vision," he thought. "Very odd. Think I'll get up and have breakfast now."

He got up, went into the kitchen and scooped some ground coffee into the drip coffee pot, added water, and turned it on. Then he went into the bathroom, pissed, and splashed water on his face.

He looked at his face in the mirror. "Did I shower yesterday?" he asked himself. "Yes, yes, I think I did, before don Fernando picked me up to go to La Chorrera. Okay, well then, I guess the next question is, do I have to shower today?" He started to hum, and made up a little song to himself. "Yes, yes, I think I do, a little shower just for you..."

Just then the phone rang.

"Hola," Dan answered cheerfully, "This is Dan. I'm not here right now, but if I call you back later, you can leave me a message."

There was a pause on the other end. "Dani?"

Dan recognized don Fernando's voice, and said, "Forgive me father, for I have sinned. It's been sixty years since my last confession."

"Dani? This is don Fernando."

"And if you act now, we'll send you, as an extra bonus, this coupon good for another free bonus."

"Dani! Stop it, this is Fernando."

"Oh alright, don Fernando. Just horsing around. What's up?"

"Are you okay?" don Fernando asked.

"Of course... are *you*?" Dan replied.

There was a pause on the other end, then an audible sigh, and then don Fernando spoke, "Dani, I just called to say thank you for meeting with Jorge Manuel yesterday. I know you did it as a favor to me, and I appreciate it. I think your words helped to focus him on the case."

"Ah, well you are very welcome, don Fernando."

"Would you like to hear the latest?"

"The latest about what?" Dan asked.

"About the case," don Fernando said.

"No," Dan replied. "I don't care about that case. I don't do that kind of work anymore."

"Well you should Dani, you're good at it," don Fernando said. "Anyway, it turns out the gringo is not a gringo..." don Fernando started to say.

"Yeah, yeah, I know," interrupted Dan, "He's Bulgarian."

There was another pause on the line... this time longer.

"How did you know that, Dani?" don Fernando said quietly.

"Well, as you said, amigo, I'm good at what I do. Now, if you'll excuse me, I haven't had breakfast yet and I am hungry."

"Breakfast? It's almost three o'clock."

"Yes, but I just got up."

"Well... can I call you tomorrow?" don Fernando asked. "I want to talk with you about this case."

"No, don Fernando, not tomorrow. Tomorrow I am going hiking. Call me the day after tomorrow."

There was another pause on the line, followed by another sigh. "Okay, my friend. The day after tomorrow. Maybe lunch or dinner?"

"Yes, yes, that would be nice," Dan said.

* * *

After don Fernando hung up the phone, he just sat at his desk staring into space and shook his head. He was worried about his friend. He knew what Dan meant by "hiking." That was his euphemism for going up into the mountains to gather more ayahuasca leaves to brew that crazy potion.

Don Fernando had not known many people who drank ayahuasca. It was an activity largely confined to indigenous tribes up in the mountains or in the jungles—tribes that kept away from any form of civilization. But the few people he had known over the years who drank it had all gone over the edge, disappeared, or had met with sudden and violent deaths. He did not want to lose his friend that way. But the one time that don Fernando had tried to talk with Dan about it, Dan had gotten very strange and it had scared don Fernando. It was a conversation that had happened in Dan's apartment, a few weeks after Dan had moved back to Panama from the States. Don Fernando had spotted a plastic bottle filled with a dirty brown liquid on Dan's kitchen counter.

"What's that?" don Fernando had innocently asked. "A science experiment?"

Dan looked over to what don Fernando was referring to, and said, "Oh that's just a little homemade medicine."

Don Fernando picked up the bottle and examined the leaves floating in the brown liquid. "Did you make this, or buy it?" he asked.

Dan walked over to don Fernando and gently took the bottle out of his hands and placed it back on the kitchen counter. "I made it."

"What is it?"

Dan gave don Fernando a totally cold look and said flatly, "It's ayahuasca."

Don Fernando felt a sting of panic. He looked at the bottle and then looked back at Dan who was still just standing there staring at him.

"Dani," he said, "you shouldn't be messing with that stuff. It's dangerous."

"No more dangerous than you thinking about hiring Giselle and putting her in charge of the police accounts receivable."

"Wha...What did you say?" don Fernando stammered.

Dan continued to stare coldly at don Fernando. "I said, no more dangerous than you thinking about hiring Giselle and putting her in charge of the police accounts receivable."

Don Fernando felt like he had been punched in the stomach. Giselle had been his mistress for many years. Despite the fact that he was happily married, don Fernando, like many married Latino men, had a mistress. Giselle had been nagging him lately for more money, and don Fernando simply didn't have it to give her, so he had been thinking about offering to put her on the payroll, let her work a few hours a week, but pay her full time wages. The problem was, he hadn't told *anyone* of his plans, not even Giselle. Don Fernando reached his hand out to the counter and grabbed it to steady himself. Dan's eyes remained fixed on don Fernando, without blinking.

"How...how did you know that?" he asked.

Dan smiled a half-smile for the first time and gestured toward the plastic bottle on the counter. "Ayahuasca told me," he said.

Don Fernando jerked his hand away from the counter, looked at the bottle and then looked at Dan, his mouth open.

"Here's the deal, mi amigo," Dan said, "You don't ask me about ayahuasca and I won't ask you about Giselle. Deal?"

Don Fernando nodded his head in agreement and said weakly, "Deal."

And don Fernando didn't mention ayahuasca again

to Dan, and Dan never mentioned Giselle again. But as a result of that conversation, don Fernando decided not to hire Giselle. He wasn't a superstitious man, but he did believe in omens. He would just have to find some other way to pay Giselle.

Chapter 5

There was a young man from Thailand
who learned about greed first-hand.
His aspirations were high,
all the way from Mumbai,
but he still ended up a dead man.

It was six days before don Fernando saw Dan again. But then, don Fernando knew better than to expect Dan to return from "hiking" in less than four or five days. But he did return, and don Fernando invited him out to lunch. By chance—or fate—this lunch occurred exactly one week after the two men had met with Jorge Manuel in La Chorrera. But today's lunch occurred in Villa Rosario. Don Fernando arranged to meet Dan at Mariscos, a small outdoor restaurant in Villa Rosario near don Fernando's office.

To don Fernando, Dan seemed dazed, as if he was emerging from a cave after hibernating. The light seemed to hurt his eyes, so they picked a table underneath the overhanging tin awning, to be in the shade. (Now... at the exact same moment that Dan was sitting down with don Fernando at Mariscos in Villa Rosario, Ricardo was walking into Las Cuñados, Miguel's restaurant in La Chorrera—but we'll get to that in a bit.)

"Dani," don Fernando was saying, "I want to talk to you about this case, the dead Asian man in the hotel, remember? I know you are not interested, but humor me."

Dan was looking at the menu, "Sure, don Fernando, talk to me... I wonder if they have camarones."

"Yes, they do, top of the next page," don Fernando said, pointing to the listing for shrimp. "Listen, Dani. When Jorge Manuel first called me about this case, I thought he was blowing it out of proportion... how is it you gringos say, making a mountain out of a gopher hill... but now I'm not so sure he isn't right."

"Yeah?" Dan said, still looking at the menu.

"Well, remember Jorge Manuel telling us that the lab in Panama City said that the tissue sample in the ice chest was unusual—that it contained both human and pig cells?"

"Uh huh," Dan said, closing the menu. "I think I will have the camarones. So what about it? I thought he sent the chest to the FBI laboratory in Bethesda, Maryland."

"He did," don Fernando said.

"Okay. So... did he get a report back?"

"Yes, and this is what is troubling. The FBI laboratory got back to him the day after they got the ice chest. They said the tissue was just animal tissue, just pig blood."

"Okay," Dan said, and looked at don Fernando. "So, what's the problem?"

"There are several problems, Dani," don Fernando explained. "First, the tissue is *not* just pig blood. The lab in Panama kept a sample of it and re-tested it. They are standing by their analysis that it is something weird that contains both human and pig cells, but it's definitely not just pig blood. Secondly, the same day that the FBI told Jorge Manuel that the tissue was just pig blood, four FBI agents showed up in La Chorrera and took the dead man."

"What? What do you mean?"

"I mean, four FBI agents showed up, flashed their badges, and claimed they were doing an investigation, and took the dead Asian's body from the morgue."

"What did they do with it?" Dan asked.

"We don't know," don Fernando answered. "They came on a U.S. government plane, put the body on the plane and flew away."

Dan looked at don Fernando. This made no sense. "Ummm don Fernando, they had no legal right to do that."

"Yes, I know, but they showed some document to the morgue attendants, and just took the body away before anyone could call Jorge Manuel."

"How do you know they were FBI?" Dan asked.

"Well, the morgue attendants said they had ID, and documents, and guns, and a plane," don Fernando said.

"They came waltzing into Panama carrying guns?" Dan asked incredulously.

"Uh huh, and never even stopped at Immigration. Flew in, took the body, and flew out in less than two hours. When Jorge Manuel found out, he called Immigration to find out what was going on, but Immigration just told him they were going to cooperate with the FBI, and that he shouldn't worry about it."

Dan looked at don Fernando and then looked away. The waiter was walking over to take their order, but Dan made a gesture with his hand to tell him they weren't ready. He was no longer hungry. He sat quietly for a moment and just thought. Don Fernando waited patiently.

Finally Dan looked up and asked, "Has anyone from the FBI talked to Jorge Manuel?"

"No, the only contact he's had was the fax report saying that the tissue in the ice chest was just pig blood."

"So the FBI doesn't know that the lab in Panama has a sample of the tissue?"

"No, they don't."

"Can you arrange a meeting with someone from that lab and you and me and Jorge Manuel? I'd like to go there and meet them face-to-face."

"Of course, I will call this afternoon. Maybe we can go tomorrow, Dani."

Dan thought a bit more, then said, "No, we should go today. Can you call now?"

Don Fernando reached into his pocket and pulled out his cell phone. "I'll call Jorge Manuel and tell him to arrange it for today," he said to Dan.

"Okay, yeah... yes, let's do it today," Dan said quietly, and looked at his hands while don Fernando punched in Jorge Manuel's phone number.

* * *

Ten minutes later, Dan and don Fernando were driving to La Chorrera to pick up Jorge Manuel. On the drive there, don Fernando updated Dan on other developments in the case.

"Jorge Manuel tracked down the two women who were at the hotel the night that Asian man was murdered," don Fernando explained.

"That's a good break," Dan said. "How was he able to do that? There must be, what... six million hookers in La Chorrera?"

Don Fernando could never tell anymore when his friend was being serious or not. He stole a glance at Dan, but Dan's expression told him nothing.

"No, Dani," he said. "La Chorrera is a clean town. Very few prostitutes."

"Right, but very nice ones," Dan said.

"Well, yes, that is true."

"So how did he find them?" Dan asked.

"Well, between me and you," don Fernando said, "he asked Jenny. She knows everyone and everything they do."

Jenny was the owner of a small, but well-respected, brothel in La Chorrera.

"Ah, yes... Jenny," said Dan. "How's she doing?"

"She is doing well, Dani. She is a smart woman, a good businesswoman."

"Yes... I know," said Dan. Dan thought back to his last girlfriend in Panama, a young woman named Magali, who used to work at Jenny's. He missed her, and wondered if she still worked for Jenny.

"Did these two hookers work for Jenny?" Dan asked.

"No," Dan said, "but Jenny knew who they were. They work out of an apartment the San Antonio neighborhood. Jenny says there are about seven girls who live in this one tiny apartment, trying to set up their own escort service. Three of these girls are immigrants from Eastern Europe... I don't know why they would come all the way here to be prostitutes. They could just do that in Europe."

"Europe has very strict tax laws," Dan explained. "Plus strict visa rules. Here, not so much. The Russian cartels bring these girls here because they can make more money off them here than in Europe."

Don Fernando stole another glance at Dan. This time he decided that Dan was being serious.

"You think there is a Russian mafia in La Chorrera?" he asked.

"Well, those three Eastern European girls didn't get over here by themselves, don Fernando—they're not that capable. So, is one or more of them from Bulgaria?"

"Yes! How did you know?"

"Just a guess, actually... Tell me more about what Jenny said."

"Well, Jenny met a couple of these girls when they applied to work for her last year. But Jenny—and I don't know if you know this—but Jenny won't hire anyone except local Panamanian women..."

"Yeah, I did know that about her," Dan said. "When I first heard that, I just assumed she was, you know... racist... but Ricardo explained to me that it's just a business decision—that Jenny feels she can control local girls more."

"Ricardo, the gringo writer?"

"Yeah."

"But how does he know this?"

"Ricardo is good friends with Jenny," Dan explained, "He is a frequent customer there."

"But he is *gay*," protested don Fernando.

"Well... yes and no, he goes both ways. But anyway, tell me more about what Jenny said."

Don Fernando gave his head a tiny shake. As long as he lives, he thought to himself, he will not understand this gay thing. He could accept it if a man was homosexual, ok... he could accept that. He didn't approve, but if a man kept it quiet, that was his business. And he certainly understood straight men who slept with many women—that was normal. But for a man to want to have sex with both men and women? That made no sense to don Fernando. He wanted to tell Dani that his friend Ricardo should make up his damn mind. But he decided to keep his opinion to himself.

"So, about a year ago, two of these girls came to see Jenny, to apply for a job. Jenny didn't hire them because they weren't local. They were both from Colombia, but Jenny was nice to them, and befriended them, gave them advice... well, you know Jenny."

"Yeah, she was keeping an eye on the competition," Dan said.

"That was probably part of it, but still, they became quasi-friends, and so when the three new blonde girls showed up this year, Jenny asked her friends where they were from..."

"I'm getting it," Dani said, interrupting don Fernando. "The Colombian girls told Jenny that this Bulgarian man brought the three girls over to work in the apartment, asked the Colombian girls to train them, and supervise them."

"Ye-yes," don Fernando stuttered. He again wanted to ask Dan how he knew all this, but Dan continued talking. "But the two girls who were at the hotel that night, they weren't Bulgarian... they were Colombian, right? Because the dead man liked Colombian women, right? And the Colombian girls, they told Jenny all this because they were bragging to her about making so much easy money off a drunk Asian man, trying to make her jealous that she didn't hire them, right?"

Don Fernando was flabbergasted. "How do you know this, Dani? Have you talked to Jorge Manuel or Jenny?"

"Ha, no... relax, mi amigo," Dan laughed, seeing don Fernando's frustration. "I'm just connecting the dots. So Jenny was pissed at the two girls for bragging, so when Jorge Manuel came sniffing around, Jenny spilled the beans. If they hadn't bragged about the drunk guy being Asian, Jorge Manuel wouldn't have learned all this. But when he asked Jenny if she knew of any prostitutes that had been servicing an Asian man once a month, she ratted the Colombian girls out."

"Basically, yes," don Fernando said. "Jorge Manuel then arrested the two Colombian girls on a pimping charge, and grilled them about the Bulgarian..."

"His name is Krasko," Dan said suddenly. He said it suddenly because he had just remembered it suddenly. That was the name the Thai man had called the Bulgarian in the vision.

"What?" don Fernando sputtered.

"His name is Krasko," Dan repeated. "I just remembered."

"Remembered? Remembered from what?!" Don Fernando was almost shouting now.

"Oh, from a dream I had," Dan said calmly. "And one of the guys with him, his name is Puii. I don't know the other guy's name. So anyway, what did the two hookers tell Jorge Manuel?"

Don Fernando wanted to stare at Dan, or shake him—he wasn't sure which—but he had to keep his eyes on the road. He gripped the steering wheel tight, took a deep breath and said, "The first time they met the Bulgarian was when he brought the three blonde girls to the apartment, and worked out details regarding their rent. But the Colombians know that the Bulgarian is pimping the girls out, because the blonde girls get a lot of business and don't speak much Spanish. The blonde girls have their own cell phones and get calls to go out. They don't do any advertising. The Colombian girls are trying to teach them some Spanish... that's how they learned that the Bulgarian man was from Bulgaria."

"Does Krasko ever use their services? Or the services of any of the other girls in the apartment?" Dan asked.

"Well, that's where it gets interesting. The Colombians told Jorge Manuel that, about six months ago, the Bulgarian called the Colombian girls and said he had a friend who liked "cinnamon girls"—that's what he calls the Colombians because of the color of their skin—so he paid the two Colombian girls to come to the Hotel de Cero to have sex with the man. He would come and pick them up and drive them to the hotel. The girls said that there were always three Asians at the hotel plus the Bulgarian. Sometimes they would have sex with all four men, and sometimes with just the man whose hotel room it was. But they said that clearly the focus of the party was for this one man who had the room. There was always liquor and everyone was having a good time."

"Hmmm, always the same two Colombians?" Dan asked.

"Almost always. By this time there were two more prostitutes living in the apartment—two girls from Brazil. The Bulgarian took these Brazilian girls over to the hotel one time, but usually he took the Colombian girls."

"So this last time it was the two original Colombian girls?" Dan asked.

"Yes."

"Are they still in custody?" Dan asked.

"No, Jorge Manuel really couldn't charge them with pimping. He just wanted to question them. So he had to let them go after two hours."

"Hmmm," said Dan. "Well, if they are stupid enough to tell the blonde girls that they were arrested, then Krasko will have them killed," Dan said calmly.

Don Fernando was silent, thinking that Dan was right, and that they needed to warn Jorge Manuel.

"Do we know anything more about this Khambang dude?" Dan asked.

"Ah yes," don Fernando said, "that is also interesting. Jorge Manuel went to the Thailand Embassy in Panama City..."

"You know, I was wondering if Thailand even had an embassy in Panama," Dan interjected.

"Well, it is one man and a secretary—a small office— just a consulado, but it is official," don Fernando explained. "But anyway, Jorge Manuel went there and explained the situation. At first the consulado didn't seem that interested. But when Jorge Manuel told him how the FBI took the body of one of their country's citizens... well, the man got upset."

"I bet he did," said Dan.

"So the consulado did some checking on this dead man. Luckily, Jorge Manuel still had the man's passport— and this Khambang Bunyasarn was rather an interesting man. He was a biologist and used to work for some Thai government agricultural agency, but he got fired last year."

"Hmm... fired for what?" Dan asked.

"Stealing."

"Stealing what?"

"That I don't know. But we'll be in La Chorrera in a few minutes and Jorge Manuel will tell us."

* * *

Jorge Manuel was waiting outside the police station in La Chorrera when don Fernando and Dan pulled up. He leaned down to the car window and said to the two men, "Our appointment in Panama City is not until 2:00, so we have a few minutes. Come inside and let's talk. Did you both get lunch?"

"No," Dan said abruptly, realizing that now he *was* hungry. "No, we... we forgot, I guess..."

"I will have the sergeant bring us some bocadillos and coffee," said Jorge Manuel said. "You can park right here," he added, pointing to the no-parking area.

Once inside, the three men went to a conference room where Khambang's suitcase and briefcase were lying on the table. The contents of his briefcase were spread out, including the dead man's passport.

"You may examine all of these freely," Jorge Manuel said. "We have checked them for fingerprints and but only found the victim's prints."

Dan picked up the passport and thumbed through it. "Interesting," he said out loud, as if talking to himself. "This guy doesn't travel for years and then suddenly, he's in and out of Thailand twice a month for the last six months... but... only to India and Panama... India, Panama, India, Panama..." Dan was flipping through the pages. "He just alternates between India and Panama... and always for only a day or two each... twice a month to India and once a month to Panama... this makes no sense... always Mumbai... never anywhere else in India... just Mumbai... not exactly a tourist town... why Mumbai?... why does Mumbai ring a bell? Hmmm."

Dan looked up as the sergeant was bringing in a tray of tiny sandwiches. "Ah, muchas gracias," Dan said to the sergeant, "Tengo hambre."

"Mucho gusto," the sergeant replied.

Another policeman brought in cups of coffee. Dan grabbed one of the sandwiches and continued to leaf through the passport. "Yup, always just a day or two in either place... He goes to Mumbai for two days, then back to Thailand... Jorge Manuel, do you have one of those big full-year calendars for this year?"

"Well, would that one do?" Jorge Manuel responded, pointing to a month-by-month calendar hanging from a tack on the wall.

"Yes, excellent," Dan said, and got up and brought the calendar back to the table. He started writing the dates of each of Khambang's passport stamps onto the calendar pages. Don Fernando and Jorge Manuel just watched him silently and nibbled on their sandwiches.

"Yeah, look at this," Dan finally said, sliding the calendar across the table. "This past six months was a strict business schedule. Look how regular the dates are: He flies to Mumbai for two days on the first week of each month; then back to Thailand; then back to Mumbai on the third week of each month, but he only stays one day; but then he flies directly from Mumbai to Panama and stays for two days; then back to Thailand; just like clockwork... He's on a fixed schedule..."

Don Fernando and Jorge Manuel flipped through the pages of the calendar looking at the dates Dan had marked.

Dan thought for a moment, then said, "Jorge Manuel, don Fernando said this man was working for the Thai government... what was his job?"

Jorge Manuel pulled a small notebook out of his shirt pocket and consulted it.

"He was a biologist with the NSTD—the Natural Science and Technology Department of Thailand's Agricultural Agency. The consulado at the embassy told me that this man worked in their animal production department."

Dan closed his eyes and asked quietly, "By any chance was he involved in developing new pig breeds?"

Jorge Manuel shot a glance at don Fernando. Don

Fernando just shrugged.

"Yes, Señor Dan, that was exactly his job."

Dan sighed, still with his eyes closed. "Was he in charge of modifying pig genetics in any way?"

"Well, Señor Dani, that's why he got fired. Thailand's official policy is against genetic modification. Khambang Bunyasarn's department was only supposed to develop new pig strains through selective breeding methods. But there was this company in Thailand from the United States, called Ravanco, that was trying to get a contract with the Thai government to grow bigger pigs by using genetic modification, but they got caught bribing some government officials. It turned out that Señor Khambang Bunyasarn had been on their payroll for years. So the NSTD fired him six months ago."

"I thought he got fired for stealing," Dan said.

"Well, what happened was that when Thailand's Ministry of Justice discovered that Ravanco had been bribing more than a dozen legislators, they seized Ravanco's accounts and all their documents. That's when they discovered that Ravanco had many scientists in different Thai agencies on their payroll, including our dead man. The Ministry of Justice understood why the legislators were being bribed, but they didn't know why the scientists were being paid. So they put them all under surveillance. Eventually they discovered that all of them, including this man, were doing scientific experiments for Ravanco on agency time, using agency animals and agency equipment. That's when they fired most of them, including Khambang Bunyasarn. After they fired him, they audited his office and discovered thousands of dollars of equipment was missing. High tech stuff, like lasers, nano-injections needles..." Jorge Manuel flipped through his notebook. "Names of things I can't pronounce. The Ministry of Justice wanted to charge him with theft, but his lawyers said he wasn't responsible for what happened to the equipment after they fired him. And they couldn't prove that he had taken it. So they never charged him."

"Hmmm," mused Dan. "Let me guess... after they fired him, this Ravanco company hired him."

"Sí, señor, exacto."

"And do you know what kind of research he was doing for Ravanco at his agency before he got fired?" Dan asked.

Jorge Manuel looked at his notebook again. "The consulado said he was growing something called chimera cells."

Dan frowned. "What are those?" he asked.

"I do not know, señor," Jorge Manuel said. The consulado just said that's what he was doing. I don't think he was supposed to tell me so much, but he was so angry that the FBI carried the body of a Thai citizen away without contacting him that he was shouting and talking a lot. But when I tried to call him back with more questions, he said he couldn't talk with me anymore."

"Ah..." Dan said. "They got to him."

"I think so, señor."

"Ok... and who are we meeting in Panama City today?"

"Her name is Doctora María José Vargas. She teaches at the University but also consults to the police laboratory if they need help. She is the one they called in when they tested the ice chest. She did the second test and confirmed what the lab had found. When you said you wanted to talk to someone at the lab, I figured she would be the most knowledgeable person to talk with."

Don Fernando looked at his watch, and said, "Speaking of which, we'd better be going."

Dan looked at his watch too, and noticed that his left hand was twitching.

"Before we go," he said, "may I use your bathroom?"

"Of course, señor," Jorge Manuel said. "First door on your right."

Dan stepped out of the conference room and into the

bathroom. He locked the door, and took a small flask from his inside pocket and took a long sip of ayahuasca. This was going to be a long afternoon.

* * *

Even with don Fernando's siren wailing, the drive from La Chorrera to Panama City took almost forty minutes. Dan sat in the back seat, closed his eyes and leaned his head back. The ayahuasca was coursing through his system. He could hear Jorge Manuel and don Fernando talking in the front seat, but the words just took on a silver shimmer, like spinning wires, and vibrated away. There was this color in the vibration, like the flash of silver and red scales of salmon thrashing in shallow water. He looked at the bubbling water. Suddenly he was standing in the jungle, stirring a large simmering cauldron of water and ayahuasca leaves. The smoke from the wood fire mixed with the pungent odor of the boiling brown liquid. He loved that smell. He watched the smoke twirl upwards. He glanced to his left. There was the human form of Khambang Bunyasarn standing upright, but clearly dead, the body propped up by a half-dozen large sticks of wood. The body appeared to be nailed to the wooden planks. It just hung there limp, arms and legs askew, like a scarecrow. Dan looked closer at the face. It was tilted slightly to one side, resting on the end of one of the wooden sticks, eyes closed, its lips sewn shut with thick jute thread.

Dan put down the wooden paddle he had been stirring the ayahuasca with, and walked up to the corpse.

"If you could talk," Dan said, "what would you say?"

The corpse's lips didn't move, but Dan heard the reply, "They took my money."

"They took your life, dead man," Dan replied.

"Yeah, that too," the corpse replied.

"Why?"

"They didn't need me anymore."

Dan shrugged and walked back to the cauldron,

61

picked up the wooden paddle, and started stirring the bubbling mixture again. Over his shoulder, he asked the corpse: "What did they need you for originally?"

"My children," came the reply. "They wanted my children."

Dan furrowed his brow and then turned to look at the corpse again. But it was gone. There was just jungle all around him. He shrugged again, and gave the ayahuasca another stir.

* * *

"Dani, Dani, wake up, we are here." Don Fernando was jostling Dan's shoulder. Dan opened his eyes. They were in Panama City, parked in front of the Ministry of Justice's Forensic Laboratory.

"Yeah, yeah okay," Dan said, forcing himself out of his reverie. His neck felt stiff from being at a strange angle. He climbed out of the car and stretched his arms and massaged the back of his neck.

"What time is it?" he asked.

"Almost two," said Jorge Manuel. "Follow me."

They walked into the building, and both Jorge Manuel and don Fernando showed their badges and ID cards to the guard and told him that Dan was with them. Jorge Manuel then led the group up to the fifth floor where one of the crime laboratories was located. He led them down a hallway to a small room that looked to Dan like a laboratory classroom. Through the window in the door, he could see several tall tables with jars of chemicals on them but no chairs around them. Dr. María José Vargas was writing something on the blackboard when Jorge Manuel knocked on the door. She turned and looked, and waved them in.

Since there were no chairs, the three men gathered around Dr. Vargas as Jorge Manuel introduced themselves. Dan gave Dr. Vargas a quick look. She was about 45 years old, dressed conservatively, black hair—with a few light streaks of gray—pulled back in a tight bun. A simple necklace but no other jewelry. She was attractive but had a professorial, no-nonsense look about her, almost stern.

"Do any of you have a molecular biology background?" Dr. Vargas asked. The three men shook their heads no. "Genetics? ... Chemistry? ... Any science at all?" Each question was greeted with a round of quiet nay shakes. She scowled and said, "Well, then, this is going to be difficult. I don't understand why they don't teach science in school anymore. It seems like the entire human race is becoming more and more uneducated."

Dan hadn't ridden crammed into the back of don Fernando's patrol car all the way to Panama City to be lectured at. Plus, the ayahuasca was making him irritable, so he spoke up. "What are chimera cells?" he asked flatly.

Dr. Vargas looked up. At least this gringo had an intelligent question.

"A Chimera was a beast in ancient Greek mythology," she explained. "It had the head of a lion, sometimes three heads, the body of a goat, and a serpent's tail. But in genetics, that word refers to an organism that has cells from different zygotes."

"What's a zygote?" Jorge Manuel asked.

"It's a fertilized egg," Dan said impatiently, and then Dan asked, "Can you give me an example of a chimera, Dr. Vargas? Something I could see in everyday life?"

"In the laboratory there are many examples, but they are all under a microscope," Dr. Vargas said. "An example that you might see out of the laboratory? Well, think of conjoined twins. Most of them are from the same zygote that split and formed two zygotes. So, they are identical twins, with the same DNA. But the split was not perfect, so the two bodies are fused. That is *not* a chimera. But what if they were conjoined fraternal twins? That is, two different zygotes that fused? Sometimes that fusion is not perfect, and you end up with conjoined twins, each with different DNA. It's rare, but you could see it. It's a single organism—sort of—but it's an organism with cells from two different zygotes. Even rarer, one in several billion, would be two different zygotes that fused after fertilization but before implementation, and the fusion was perfect, so that you ended up with one person, who had two different sets of DNA in them. They would look and act the same as anyone else, and unless they had some complicated DNA tests, you would never know, but that person would be a true chimera."

"But what's a zygote?" Jorge Manuel asked again.

Dan really wanted to understand this chimera thing, and he didn't want to be slowed down by Jorge Manuel's questions. But when he looked at don Fernando's face, he realized that neither don Fernando nor Jorge Manuel was following what Dr. Vargas was saying.

"Look," Dan said to both men. "A woman makes an egg, right?" He made a circle with his left forefinger and thumb. "And a man makes sperm, right? And when they have sex, if they don't use protection, that sperm can penetrate that egg, right?" Dan straightened the forefinger of his right hand and pushed it back and forth through the circle of his left hand. "That egg is fertilized, right? That fertilized egg is called a zygote!"

Dan saw both don Fernando's and Jorge Manuel's eyes widen in shock. He looked at his hands and realized he was making the universal hand gesture for fucking. He didn't care. He turned to Dr. Vargas and muttered, "Visual aids." He then continued talking to don Fernando and Jorge Manuel. "That zygote is just one cell, a single cell... but it can start dividing, and it can attach itself to the woman's uterus, and then you know what happens?"

Both don Fernando and Jorge Manuel shook their heads no.

"You start paying child support!" he said. He heard Dr. Vargas muffle a laugh. Good, Dan thought, she can laugh. He continued talking to the two men. "She gets pregnant. Well, what the doctor is saying is that, well, suppose you had two different fertilized eggs, but somehow you mixed them together..."

Dan stopped suddenly. He had been so engrossed with the example of the fraternal conjoined twins that he had momentarily forgotten that the ice chest contained some mixture of DNA from cells from a human and a pig. He turned to Dr. Vargas, gave her a quick cold look and asked,

"The cells in that ice chest have nothing to do with twins, do they?"

"No, they don't," she said. "Let me explain. The current chimera research is for growing body parts. The theory is that we could grow human body parts—for use in transplant cases—by implanting human stem cell material into a different animal, like pigs. We're years, maybe decades away, from perfecting the process, but we're making progress."

"How much progress?" Dan asked.

"We can grow pancreases in rats that are made up entirely of cells from mice," Dr. Vargas explained. "We can alter the DNA of a rat zygote so that it cannot grow a rat pancreas, and then inject it with stem cells from a mouse pancreas, so that basically the rat grows a pancreas that works, but it's really a mouse pancreas. The hope is that one day we can grow human livers, and hearts, and other organs in pigs, and then harvest those organs for transplant into humans."

Dan heard Jorge Manuel gasp. Dan knew that what Dr. Vargas was saying was beginning to sink into the police chief's Catholic mind. Dan felt that Jorge Manuel was going to say something opinionated, so he held up his hand and signaled him not to. Dr. Vargas also probably intuited something similar, because she added, "The average wait for a transplant is over three years. Most people die while they are waiting. A pig can reach full size—over 200 pounds—in less than nine months. We could literally save thousands of lives a year if we could perfect a way to grow human organs in pigs."

"Is that what you found in the ice chest?" don Fernando asked, "some type of human body part grown in a pig?"

"No... no it wasn't..." Dr. Vargas said, and for the first time Dan discerned a sense of worry, almost panic, in her. "That is the problem... When the lab first examined the ice chest, they found a smear of blood with some tissue on one of the inside walls. When they examined the blood under a microscope, they saw different types of cells, some that looked like human cells and some that looked like cells from the Sus, or pig, genus. What bothered the lab technicians was that some of these cells were fused together. The blood was closer to pig blood than human blood, but some of the cells were very human-looking. So they sent a sample to my laboratory at the University. They assumed that the ice chest was used for transporting human body parts for transplants. But this process I described for actually growing human organs in pigs is still decades away, so they didn't know really what they were looking at. But we did DNA analysis at our lab..." She stopped. She seemed to be struggling to find the right words.

"Is there somewhere we can go and all sit down to discuss this?" Dan asked. "I have the sense this conversation may take a while."

"Yes, that's a good idea," Dr. Vargas said, relieved to have a break. "Follow me."

She led them out of the laboratory and down a hallway to a small conference room with a table and chairs in front of a large window. They all took seats, with Dr. Vargas sitting at the head of the table.

"So, doctor," Dan started. "You were saying..."

Dr. Vargas took a breath and started: "If you were to grow a human liver, for example, in a pig, and harvest that liver and test the DNA in that liver—it would be human DNA, even though it was grown in a pig. The tissue that we found in that ice chest was different. It looked like human tissue, but it had parts of pig DNA mixed in it. We had never seen anything like this before. We used an electron microscope to examine the DNA—and the normal double helix had all these pig DNA sections spliced in. At first, we thought it might be some random mutation, but the splices were too organized. There were these rings of pig DNA strands at regular intervals in the helix..."

"Rings?" Dan asked, "What do you mean rings?"

"Well," Dr. Vargas said, looking at Dan, "you know that the structure of the double helix is like? Two twisting threads, connected but held apart by nucleotides, called base pairs, that act like struts on a bridge, giving the structure shape and strength, right?" Dan nodded, and Dr.

Vargas continued. "The basic structure of the helix in the sample we examined was all human DNA, but at frequent intervals, there were these connective rings, made from pig DNA, that circled the helix and connected different base pairs... it was as if someone had wired in short circuits onto a circuit board. These rings would connect sections of DNA that normally would never connect. We don't know what the purpose of this modification was... what outcome this DNA splicing would have on the final product."

"The final product..." Dan said, and paused. "This tissue that you found... what was it from? I mean, could you tell whether it was a liver or a heart?"

"It was fetal tissue, fetal stem cells."

Dan stared at Dr. Vargas. He opened his mouth to say something, and then closed it again. He didn't want to go where his mind was going, but he had to ask. "Do you mean, doctor, that if this thing... this tissue... were to... develop into a ... a final product... it would be a person?"

"Hypothetically... yes."

"What kind of person?"

"We don't know. It had XY chromosomes, so it would be male, but that's all we could say."

Dan stared into space. Jorge Manuel raised his hand and said, "Doctor, I'm confused, I thought DNA was very tiny. How could other DNA be 'spliced' in, as you say?"

Dan interrupted him, "I'm sorry, Doctor," he said, "Is there a bathroom on this floor?"

"Yes, just down the hall."

"Thank you."

Dan got up and walked out of the room and down the hall. He found the bathroom, went in, locked the door, and splashed some water on his face. He looked at his hands. They had started twitching again. He reached into his pocket for his flask and took another sip of ayahuasca. As an afterthought, he peed. Then he returned to the conference room.

Dr. Vargas was talking, and don Fernando and Jorge Manuel were looking a bit glazed by all the information. "So you see," she was saying, "these two biopolymer strands are coiled around each other—that's what we call the double helix. And we know, from decades of research what every sequence is, that is, where in the strand every molecule or every chromosome is, so we can test portions of a strand and tell if it is human or some other animal."

Dan took his seat and just stared out the window. He wasn't listening to Dr. Vargas. He was watching Khambang Bunyasarn come through the airport carrying his ice chest. He handed the customs inspector some documents. The customs inspector looked at the documents and then glanced at the ice chest, handed the documents back to Khambang and waved him through. Dan was also looking at the ice chest. He held the image of the ice chest in his mind and looked through the walls past the blocks of dry ice. He was expecting to see a blob of some kind, something that looked like meat, maybe like a piece of liver, but that's not what he saw. He saw what looked like a series of plastic ice trays, sealed top and bottom, basically a sheet of capsules, with each capsule holding a small spoonful of reddish tissue. One of the capsules had broken and the reddish blob was stuck against the wall of the ice chest. The image faded. Dan blinked several times and looked around the conference room. Dr. Vargas was still talking. Why would there be so many samples, so many capsules? Were they each different, or the same? What did Khambang mean back in the jungle when he said that they wanted his children? What children?

"Dr. Vargas!" Dan almost shouted. The doctor looked startled. He had obviously interrupted her explanation to Jorge Manuel and don Fernando. "Oh sorry, sorry," Dan said, "but it just occurred to me. This DNA in the ice chest—it's human DNA right? I mean, it has to be *from a human*, from a person, even if it has been modified, right?"

"Yes," she answered.

"If we supplied you with a tissue sample from someone, could you test your sample and see if the DNA matched? I mean, matched minus the pig parts?"

"Of course."

"Jorge Manuel, you still have the bloody cloth from the body? You know, the cloth that was stuck... well, the one with blood on it?"

"Sí, señor."

"Can you get that cloth to the good doctor? Like maybe have someone bring it here today?"

Jorge Manuel looked at Dan and then at don Fernando. Don Fernando just nodded his head yes.

"Sí, señor," Jorge Manuel said, and reached for his cell phone.

"Good, thank you, yes..." Dan turned toward the doctor. "Doctor Vargas, let me say something that we should have said at the very beginning. This is a murder case. And it's a very sensitive case. It's important that neither you nor your staff talk to anyone about this case... And the tissue sample that you have, can you guard it carefully? Do you have a secure place to store it, like in a safe?"

"It will be secure in my laboratory at the University."

"Okay, good... good... let me see if I can sort this out in my mind. And pardon my for talking out loud... but I'm not sure I understand the difference between fetal tissue and stem cells... which exactly was this tissue you examined?"

"These were what we call embryonic stem cells but, again, it was more than that. It was as if these basic stem cells, the ones with the modified DNA, were either floating in the same blood as other human and pig cells, or actually in some type of tissue that was either human or pig... The sample was too small to tell us which. But the embryonic cells that I was describing, they were stem cells, capable of becoming any and all parts of a human."

"And when you say this sample is small, how much of a sample do you have left?" Dan asked.

"After all the testing we've done, we're down to two microscope slides. We could see if there is any more on the sides of the ice chest if you would bring that back to us."

"Unfortunately, it's gone," Dan said. He thought of the FBI laboratory in Maryland, and blamed himself for suggesting that Jorge Manuel send it there.

Jorge Manuel hung up his cell phone. "They're bringing the cloth," he said to Dan. "They should be here within the hour."

"Okay," Dan said. "Doctor, what the police are bringing is a blood-soaked rag. It contains the blood of a murder victim. My hunch is that the DNA in the blood will match—if that's the right word—that it will match the DNA in the tissue sample. Whether it does or not doesn't really help us solve the case, but it might fill in some gaps."

"One thing I forgot to mention," Dr. Vargas said, "was the percentage of these human cells. Our sample was small, but about 80% of the cells in the blood were just regular pig cells. Only 10% were human cells."

"And the other 10%?" Dan asked.

"Well, they were the fused cells I mentioned. They appeared to be a pig cells that were conjoined with human cells."

Dan looked at Dr. Vargas questioningly, "I'm missing something. What does that mean?"

"Well," she said, "that never happens in nature. There would be no reason, no catalyst, no way for the cells of two different species to naturally fuse like that... at least no way we know of... Maybe some chemical agent was used, or some fusing technique, but... well, like I said, we've never seen anything like this. One of the lab technicians said it looked like the human cells were attacking the pig cells, but of course we had no way to observe any activities because these cells were dead."

"Ahhh," said Dan, and closed his eyes, and let his head roll back. Suddenly, his mind was filled with the image of Goya's painting of Saturn—the ancient god who ate his own children. A shiver ran through his body. He opened his eyes and smiled at don Fernando and Jorge Manuel who were just staring at him. "Sorry," he said, "It's just such a strange case. Doctor, are you going to be here for the next hour? If so, we'll leave you in peace and go downstairs to the lobby to wait for our delivery. We thank you so much for your time and expertise."

"I'll be here," she smiled. Thank *you* for your interest in our work." It was the first time Dan had seen her smile. He began to realize how attractive she actually was.

"Come gentlemen," Dan said to Jorge Manuel and don Fernando. "Let's go wait downstairs. We have much to discuss."

And all three men rose and left the room.

Chapter 6

There was a young man from Thailand
who dabbled in things that were banned.
His preoccupation was strange,
his DNA rearranged,
but it all just slipped through his hands

Downstairs in the lobby, the three men found a quiet corner to talk while they waited for one of Jorge Manuel's men to bring the bloody cloth to them.

"I didn't follow everything Dr. Vargas was saying," Jorge Manuel said. Don Fernando shook his head in agreement.

"Nor did I," Dan confessed, "But, basically... it doesn't matter. What I said last week when we were together is still true: It doesn't matter *what* was in the ice chest, because whatever it was, it was just a *motive*. Maybe it was something valuable, something worth killing that guy for... or maybe it wasn't. Maybe they just wanted his money. But it doesn't matter. You still have a dead body... well, you *had* a dead body before the FBI took it away... and you have these three suspects: Krasko, Puii, and the second Asian guy..."

"Who? What?" exclaimed Jorge Manuel.

"Dani thinks those are the names of two of the men," don Fernando explained to Jorge Manuel.

Jorge Manuel started to ask, "But how...?" but don Fernando just gestured to him not to bother asking.

"The links to these three guys," Dan continued, "are the hookers. I would suggest re-arresting those two Colombian girls and the three blonde hookers... it's probably for their own safety anyway... but somehow locking them up until you can arrest the Bulgarian and his two partners. It's the Bulgarian who is the top dog here. He's the one who originally shot this Khambang dude..." Dan stood up. He was on a roll now. He started pointing into the air. "And Puii is the only witness to that... So, actually, this Puii guy is the most important link! We need to arrest him and keep him separate from Krasko. Puii's the one we need to flip. If we can get him to testify against Krasko, we can nail him... Yeah, we need this Puii dude. He's the one who can explain the Mumbai connection too..."

"Señor Landes," Jorge Manuel said, "I'm so confused."

Dan looked at Jorge Manuel, and then laughed, and sat down. He realized that he must have sounded like a crazy man, rambling on like that.

"Sorry, Jorge Manuel," Dan said, and smiled. "Let me try to explain what I think is going on: This Khambang fellow is doing experiments with human tissue in Thailand, being paid by this Ravanco company. He gets fired from his government job, so he moves his operation to Mumbai, or rather... Ravanco moves Khambang's operation to Mumbai. We know this because he's still on the Ravanco payroll, and someone is paying him to fly to Mumbai twice a month. He flies there the first week of every month just to check on something. He stays two days and then flies back to Thailand. But on the third week of every month, he flies back, only stays a day, and then flies directly to Panama. Don't you see? This second trip each month is to pick something up from his laboratory or factory or whatever it is in Mumbai, pack it in dry ice, and then deliver it here in Panama to this Bulgarian named Krasko. Now we don't know what it is that he's delivering, but he has to have some papers to get it through Customs... but it doesn't matter what it is, because we know it's something valuable. He delivers it to Krasko. Krasko tests it, and if it meets his approval, they pay Khambang and bring him some hookers as a reward. Only for some reason, this trip was his last trip. We don't know why. Maybe the stuff he brought wasn't good enough, or maybe it was the final shipment—doesn't matter. But for whatever reason, Krasko and his buddies were done with him, so they spiked his drink and shot him, trying to pass it off like an overdose. But they fucked that up, and he bled all over the bed…”

“That’s true,” Jorge Manuel said, “If he had not bled, Dr. Navarro would have said he died of natural causes and no one would have known.”

“Right,” Dan said, and then added, “We don’t know if Krasko lives in La Chorrera or Panama City or whether he lives in Panama at all. Panama could just be a meeting point… That’s why we need to get those five girls into custody. We need to find out where Krasko is and more importantly, where this guy Puii is. Puii is our best… our only witness… We’ve got to find him…”

“Dani,” don Fernando chimed in, “I have a question. Why did the FBI want the body?”

Dan paused and thought for a bit. “That’s a good question, don Fernando, I don’t know… That doesn’t make any sense to me… unless they were telling the truth…”

“The truth?” don Fernando asked.

“That they really were doing an investigation… that they somehow wanted the body because of their own investigation into this crime… but even that doesn’t make sense… I don’t know… I just don’t know… you’d think if they were doing an investigation, they would have contacted Jorge Manuel…” Dan looked at Jorge Manuel. “They knew it was you who shipped the ice chest to them, right?”

“Sí, señor.”

“And you told them it was in the room with the dead man?”

“Sí…”

“And you gave them Khambang’s name?”

“Sí, and passport number,” said Jorge Manuel.

“Yeah…” Dan said, shaking his head, “Makes no sense to me… But why don’t you follow up with an inquiry… a letter protesting the removal of the body… and ask them for an explanation? Of course, don’t tell them anything about what we know. Don’t mention Dr. Vargas or the lab here. Just pretend that all you know is that you had a body and an ice chest and now you have nothing, and so you can’t investigate this death. See what they say. But before you do that, let’s pick up those five girls. Once you arrest them, keep them separate from each other—don't let them see each other. Interview them one at a time; threaten the Colombian girls with being an accessory to a murder and threaten to deport the blond girls... no wait, that won't scare them... Threaten the blond girls with jail time. Tell them how horrible the Panamanian prisons are... We've got to find this Puii guy... I wonder where he lives... don Fernando, we're going to need search warrants to search the girls' cell phones... maybe they have laptops too..."

"No problem, Dani. I'll call my brother-in-law."

"Your brother-in-law?" asked Dan, "Why?"

"His brother-in-law is Chief Justice Ortega," smiled Jorge Manuel.

"Really?" Dan said. "I didn't know that! That's fucking convenient!"

"Very convenient," don Fernando said.

"What else? What else?" Dan pondered out loud. "Hmmm, Jorge Manuel, maybe you can find out what documents Khambang used to get the ice chest through Customs so easily... He was a frequent flyer there... What else?" Dan closed his eyes. A vision of miles and miles of slums appeared in his mind. Tiny shanty houses with tin roofs and overbearing heat and stench. It was Mumbai. "I guess I'll try and do some research on Mumbai," he muttered. He opened his eyes. Jorge Manuel and don Fernando staring at him strangely. "Yes?" Dan asked, "What is it?"

"Uh, Dani," don Fernando said, "You closed your eyes about twenty minutes ago, and said something about Mumbai, and you were suddenly asleep. At least, we thought you were asleep, but then we couldn't wake you. We were worried that maybe you had a stroke or something. We were about to call an ambulance."

"Really?" Dan looked at his hands. "No, I feel okay. I must have been just very tired," he said with a smile. "When I get tired, I just... sort of nod off."

"Yes, that must be it," said don Fernando suspiciously.

Dan looked at his watch. He really had been out for twenty minutes. His last memory was of looking at the slums in Mumbai that seemed to stretch for hundreds of miles. How odd, he thought.

Just then a policeman came into the lobby holding a sealed evidence bag. Jorge Manuel stood up and went over and greeted him. Don Fernando and Dan stayed seated in the corner. While Jorge Manuel was talking to the officer, don Fernando leaned over and whispered to Dan, "You need to be careful with the things you consume, Dani."

Dan looked at his friend, frowned but nodded. "You may be right, amigo... you may be right."

Jorge Manuel came back over to the corner with the evidence bag. "I'm going to take this up to Dr. Vargas," he said. "I'll be right back." Both Dan and don Fernando nodded.

Dan sat quietly, lost in thought. Don Fernando looked at Dan's face and noticed how worried Dan looked. Finally don Fernando asked, "Is there something you are not telling us, Dani?"

"About what?"

"About this case."

"Oh... well, it's very strange, don Fernando, very strange. You know how I like to connect the dots. It's like watching different patterns arrange themselves and then re-arrange themselves in my head. Usually I'm pretty good at it. But this case... some of the patterns, when I connect them, are a bit scary."

"What do you mean, Dani?"

"Well, for instance, Krasko is Bulgarian, you know, a Russian satellite. But he's here in Panama, close to the United States... but once a Bulgarian, always a Bulgarian, I think. I don't know where his allegiances are. Khambang is Thai. Thais are not fans of communists, given the whole Vietnam War history... but he's doing business with a Bulgarian. But he's doing it here in Panama. And, he's doing it as an employee of Ravanco, which Jorge Manuel says is a U.S. company, but we really don't know that. Companies are so international now—they're like their own countries. We know that the FBI clearly knew who Khambang was, because they rushed down here and took the body, but why they wanted the body, we don't know. Do they know about Krasko too? Khambang was delivering something important to Krasko, something from halfway around the world... but why here? It's not something that was going to stay here. Krasko was going to take it somewhere else, but where? Certainly not back to Bulgaria—If that were the case, Khambang would have met him in Greece or Istanbul to do the trade. No, the package, whatever it was, was either going north or south from Panama... South doesn't make any sense, so it had to be going north to the United States. Ah it's all so crazy, don Fernando, it makes my head hurt..." Dan looked at don Fernando, and said, "But to answer your question, what scares me, and what I haven't said out loud, is that there are too many international players, too many ruthless people. You know, I like Jorge Manuel—he's a good kid—and La Chorrera is a nice town. But these guys, don Fernando, these guys are big time... bribing politicians in Thailand, assassinating couriers in hotels, bringing in hookers from Bulgaria, being watched by the FBI... the scale is just too big for Jorge Manuel... or you... or me... to handle. We need to be careful."

Don Fernando let Dan's words sink in. He hadn't looked at the situation in quite that light before, but now he saw what Dan meant. He leaned back in his chair and pursed his lips.

"Should we tell Jorge Manuel?" he asked Dan.

"Tell him what? To be careful? No, let's just work closely with him and keep our eyes open."

"Okay, Dani..." don Fernando said.

A few minutes later, Jorge Manuel came back downstairs.

"Dr. Vargas said she would try to have the results for us tomorrow afternoon," he said.

"Good," said don Fernando, "Let's get back to La Chorrera."

They all went outside and climbed back into don Fernando's patrol car. Dan sat in the back seat as he had previously. He was quiet all the way back, just thinking... thinking about rings, and circles, and patterns....

Chapter 7

Another young man from Thailand
thought he could run his own scam.
His plan was sure-fire
but the results were quite dire
and soon he will join the first man.

Speaking of rings and things that travel in circles... Ricardo's life was quite different from Dan's, and yet in some ways their lives were interconnected... as if their fates were unfolding on intersecting planes, orbiting at a different speed, with different destinies, yet each on a trajectory that crossed paths every eon or so, like earth and Halley's comet.

Many of us... in fact, most of us... believe that we are captains of our own ships, masters of our destiny, sailors navigating our own lives. Ricardo, on the other hand, felt that he was simply a witness to his own fate, a mere passenger, albeit cognizant and responsible, but still, a passenger on the shooting star that was his life. He was, as he liked to say, "only along for the ride."

And naturally, of course, Ricardo hadn't planned on getting involved with this Khambang Bunyasarn affair. In fact, he was completely ignorant of the dead Thai man— didn't know a thing about him. It was simply pure fate that made him decide to take the bus from Villa Rosario to La Chorrera exactly one week after Dan and Jorge Manuel and don Fernando had all had lunch at Los Cuñados.

It was true that Ricardo often told Dan that Los Cuñados was his favorite restaurant in La Chorrera. In fact, Ricardo made it a point to eat there several times a month, but it wasn't the food that brought him there. It was Miguel. Ricardo and Miguel had a long history together, beginning some ten years or so ago when Ricardo had first moved to Panama. He and Miguel had been lovers then; now they were just friends, but close friends. Ricardo considered Miguel to be his best friend, and his only confidant in Panama.

And so it was that on that bright and sunny midday, just a week after Dan and Jorge Manuel and don Fernando had sat down to eat at Los Cuñados in La Chorrera, that Ricardo entered Los Cuñados. And this—as mentioned—occurred at the exact same moment that Dan and don Fernando had just entered Mariscos restaurant in Villa Rosario and were selecting a table underneath the overhanging tin awning, because the light seemed to be hurting Dan's eyes...

"Ah, mi viejo amigo," Miguel said as Ricardo walked through the door. "What a wonderful surprise to see you."

Ricardo smiled, and the two men gave each other the traditional Panamanian embrace of old friends. "It's good to see you too, my friend."

"What brings you to La Chorrera today?" Miguel asked.

"Well, you know, you having this nice restaurant, and it being noon, and me being hungry... I don't know, Miguel, but somehow they all seemed to mesh," Ricardo joked. "How's business?"

"Ah, amigo, you know the restaurant business— nothing but headaches."

Miguel complained constantly about the restaurant. But in reality, he made a good living at it. Ricardo understood this about his friend, and always allowed him the first five or ten minutes of any conversation to vent about the trials and tribulations of being a restaurant owner/manager/cook/ waiter. Ricardo had developed the habit years ago of always asking Miguel, early in any get-together, how business was, in order to get the complaints out of the way.

"The price of fish keeps going up," Miguel was saying. "It's insane! We have the Atlantic on one side and the Pacific on the other side, and I can't get affordable fish! I can't raise my menu prices or customers will complain. Customers come here for our fish and our shrimp because we only serve the best, but they don't want to spend more than they pay at the worst fast-food restaurant in town. The fishermen keep raising their prices because the government keeps restricting how they can fish. I'm being squeezed in the middle!"

"Ha," Ricardo said as he sat down at a corner table. "Just raise the price of the fish, Miguel. People will pay. Especially the gringos."

"Speaking of gringos," Miguel said, "I think your friend Dan Landes came here for the first time last week. He is the one who is the friend of don Fernando, right? The gringo you described as having hair the color of beach sand?"

"Probably," said Ricardo, opening the menu. "He's close buddies with don Fernando, that's for sure. I've always told him this was my favorite restaurant."

"Well, I think he was here on official business," Miguel said.

"Oh?" asked Ricardo. "How so?"

"Well he was here with don Fernando and Jorge Manuel, our police chief. Whenever I see two police chiefs meeting together, I always assume that it is about official business."

One of Miguel's other traits, Ricardo knew, was that he loved to gossip. He was discrete with whom he gossiped, but because of his restaurant business, he was an amazing source of information. Ricardo, on the other hand, didn't care much about gossip. He lived alone in Villa Rosario and spent his time writing, but as with the complaints about restaurant business, Ricardo was willing to listen to Miguel's gossip. After all, they were friends.

"Well, that's possible," Ricardo said as he looked through the menu. "Dan is a retired cop, so it makes sense. Remember last year, when don Fernando brought Dan over here to help catch that crazy man who murdered that muchacho in the bathhouse? Remember? They even got *me* involved in that shit!"

"Sí, I remember it quite well. It was very scary to have a murder in my favorite bathhouse," Miguel said. "And maybe that's why the three men were meeting together. I think there was another murder here in town recently."

"Well, that's not unusual, is it?" Ricardo asked, "I

mean, La Chorrera is a big town. I think I read, just the other day, how some guy killed his wife when he caught her in bed with some other guy."

"True, but this case must be unusual because don Fernando was here. Jorge Manuel would not have brought don Fernando in unless it was an important murder."

"Hmmm. True," Ricardo said. "What is the special today, Miguel?"

"Corvina al ajillo," Miguel said. "It's very good. I couldn't hear much of what they were saying, but when I was serving them lunch, I caught enough of the conversation to know it was serious."

"I'll have that then. I like corvina," Ricardo said, closing the menu. "And maybe a glass of white wine with that."

"Of course," said Miguel. "Anyway, I thought of you when I was eavesdropping on them."

"Really? Why?" asked Ricardo.

"Because evidently this crime happened at the Hotel de Cero."

"Never heard of it," Ricardo said.

"It's a little place over in El Coco Barrio neighborhood," said Miguel.

"So why would that remind you of me?" Ricardo asked.

"Well, remember your old friend Marco, that cute boy who used to work for me?"

"Yes, of course I do," Ricardo said, suddenly interested.

"Well, he works there now."

"Really? Huh...what does he do there?"

"He is a manager there."

"Really? Well, now, that is good information, Miguel. Hmm, I haven't seen Marco in over a year... no, maybe two years. Hmm. Hotel de Cero you say. Where exactly is it?"

"Down the street from the Catholic Church," said Miguel.

"Oh shit, Miguel, there's a Catholic Church on every corner. That doesn't help me."

"Ha, true. Well, you know Calle 42A Norte, down the road from here?"

"Yes."

"There's a bus that runs from the big gas station where Calle 42A Norte starts, and it runs all the way to Calle San José. Well, about two blocks after Calle 42A Norte becomes Calle San José, that's where the hotel is."

"Hmmm," hummed Miguel. "Very interesting." He looked at his watch. He might have time to swing by there today before he caught a bus back to Villa Rosario.

"I know what you are thinking, my gray fox," Miguel said slyly.

"Well... of course you do," Ricardo said, and smiled.

*   *   *

An hour later, after finishing his meal, Ricardo did take the bus down Calle 42A Norte, and found the Hotel de Cero, and walked through the front entrance. He felt a bit of anxiety in doing so. After all, it had been a long time since he had seen Marco, almost two years. There had been a time when Marco was his "protegido," as they say in Spanish... meaning protégé, as they say in both English and French... but in the gay world, it was a term that meant a younger man, usually a much younger man—usually a very cute much younger man—whom an older gay man takes "under his wing" so to speak, meaning, pays for his meals and vacations, in exchange for sexual favors. Marco used to work for Miguel, as a waiter, when Ricardo first met him... but that was years ago... and Ricardo had taken young Marco under his wing... and under his arms... back then, but their vacations to various gay resorts in Panama were also years ago, so Ricardo was not sure how Marco would react upon seeing him.

But Marco seemed happy to see Ricardo, and left several gringos standing in the check-in line at the reservation desk to rush out and greet Ricardo. Ricardo made him go back and attend to his guests while he waited patiently in one of the lobby chairs until Marco finished.

Finally Marco was done with those guests, and he came over and sat down beside Ricardo.

"Mi amigo," Marco said. "It's so good to see you. How... how did you find me here?"

"Miguel told me you were working here," Ricardo said.

"Ah... Miguel... I have not seen him in... well, like forever...I still feel bad for quitting him in such a lurch..." Marco said. "How is he?"

"He's doing fine," Ricardo said. "Don't worry about him. How are you doing? You look great."

"Gracias, mi amigo, I am well. The job is difficult, but I seem to be okay here."

"Good, good, Marco. I always knew you'd do well," Ricardo said.

More new guests started to come in the front door.

"Ah, amigo," Marco apologized, looking at the new guests. "This is our busy hour, I'm sorry."

"Tranquilo, mi amigo," said Ricardo, "When's your next day off?"

"Tomorrow," said Marco.

"Well, come to Villa Rosario and have lunch with me," Ricardo suggested.

"It would be a pleasure," said Marco.

"Meet me at El Balcón at noon?" Ricardo suggested, naming his favorite restaurant in Villa Rosario.

"Sí, mucho gusto, mi amigo," Marco said, standing up to go take care of the new guests.

"See you tomorrow," Ricardo said, also standing up to leave.

Ricardo was smiling to himself as he walked out of the hotel. He was looking forward to the following day.

* * *

And, speaking of the following day: On the following day, Puii was feeling very nervous. Krasko had left Panama with the shipment of seed tissue as usual, but he had not returned yet. He had always returned within five days, with enough money to pay both Puii and Rune, but now it had been twelve days. Krasko had only texted him one time, saying his return would be delayed a week, but had given no explanation. Krasko had just told them both to sit tight until he returned.

Basically, Puii didn't trust Krasko... or rather, Puii trusted that Krasko would always look after Krasko's own interest first. But Puii knew that Krasko needed him. Without Puii, Krasko had no way to replicate the seed tissue that Khambang had been bringing over. Krasko was smart; he was a good enforcer; he knew a lot of people who had connections, power, and most importantly, money. But Krasko didn't know dog shit about science. As long as Krasko needed him, Puii was safe. And so was Rune. Puii needed a lab assistant and, yes, Rune could be replaced. But why bother? Puii would just have to find another lab assistant. Rune knew his job. More importantly, he knew how to keep his mouth shut.

Puii had worked for Khambang for years at the Natural Science and Technology Department in Thailand. He had never liked Khambang, but he always pretended he did, because Khambang was his boss, and—Puii had to acknowledge—Khambang was brilliant. Brilliant, but money-hungry. He was always complaining about not being paid enough for his work. Just like any diva, Puii had always thought—they never think they're appreciated enough.

It was Puii who had introduced Khambang to Krasko, and it was Krasko who hooked Khambang up with Ravanco, and it was Ravanco that finally paid Khambang the big bucks—money that Khambang never thought fit to share with Puii. But luckily, Khambang had gotten fired, and then Krasko had to arrange for Ravanco to pay Puii as well. Puii was never clear what Krasko's relationship with Ravanco was—Krasko wasn't an employee, but more like a supplier, and occasionally a competitor. When Krasko became dissatisfied with the amount of money that Ravanco was funneling to him, Krasko threatened to sell Khambang's product to China. That got Ravanco's attention, and they doubled the payments. Life was good when they were all in Thailand—lots of money and lots of whores—although Puii could never understand why Ravanco simply didn't kill

Krasko. They really didn't need him—Khambang was already on their payroll. But once Ravanco got caught bribing those senators, and especially once Khambang got fired... well, *then* Ravanco did need Krasko, and then they were stuck with him.

Puii checked his cell phone again. Still nothing. He went into the next room and peered through the window of his "growing room." The incubators with all the tissues all seemed to be doing well, filling up nicely. He went back into the other room and sat on the couch and thought: If Krasko was going to betray him, how would he do it? Maybe he had another chemist in the states who could grow tissue? But then Krasko would have had to have taken some of the seed tissue, and Puii always made sure he could account for every gram of that. Or maybe Krasko had simply decided that he had made enough money off of the operation. After all, they had been running it for over a year. Puii had almost a million dollars hidden in an offshore account, very expertly arranged and managed by Mossack Fonseca. Krasko must have twice that, maybe more, Puii thought. But why would Krasko decide he had enough money when their most valuable shipment yet was right behind this laboratory door? No, it made no sense that Krasko would bail out now. This current shipment would be worth at least five million dollars once it was fully grown. And it would take at least six trips back and forth to the states to deliver all of it. No, Puii reasoned that he still had plenty of time. And he needed that time, to develop his own deal...

Long before Ravanco fucked up and got caught bribing senators, Puii had started cultivating a relationship with Afzaal Minhas at the Institute for BioGenetics in Pakistan. Originally, Puii was just looking for job opportunities, but he and Afzaal had hit it off. Over the months prior to Khambang's being fired, Puii had shared just enough of the scope of Khambang's work that Afzaal saw the true potential, both in terms of science and money, but mostly in terms of money. Puii had been careful never to share any formulas, because he knew how smart Afzaal was, but they had talked about forming a partnership, and maybe doing parallel work to Khambang's in Pakistan. But then, Khambang got fired.

At first Puii thought he would just take some of the seed tissue samples he had pilfered from Khambang and move to Pakistan to work with Afzaal. But then Krasko offered him so much money to move, first to Mumbai, and then to Panama, that Puii couldn't refuse. He had to put Afzaal on the back burner.

But over the past three months, Puii's suspicions about Krasko had grown, and so he had renewed his relationship with Afzaal, first by email, and then by an in-person visit. Puii had told Krasko that he was flying back to Mumbai to check on the lab, which he did in fact do, but then he took a quick side trip to Karachi, Pakistan, and had dinner with Afzaal. Because Afzaal was from the Baloch tribe, he had strong ties to the Pakistani government, and the government was *very* interested in the potential of Puii's tissue samples... *very* interested. Afzaal said they might pay triple what Ravanco was paying. Puii didn't know if, or how, he could do it... but even if he and Afzaal could sell just half of the current product in the growing room to the Pakistan government, then both he and Afzaal could split at least 15 million dollars, and he could retire—he could retire as an extremely rich man. Plus, Puii liked the idea of cutting Krasko out of the picture. He knew Krasko would do the exact same thing to him if it was in Krasko's best interest to do so. He had seen the easy manner in which Krasko had decided to kill Khambang once Puii informed him that he had been able to replicate Khambang's seed tissue and could now grow their own formative product without any more deliveries from Khambang. "Good," was all Krasko had said. "Then we can dispense with Khambang." It was said simply as a cold fact, nothing more.

Of course, Khambang never figured out that Puii had been growing formative tissue from replicated seed tissue. Puii, Rune, and Krasko had been extremely careful never to let that slip. Khambang had just assumed that Krasko was only a middleman, a courier who would deliver the seed tissue to Ravanco in the states. Khambang had no idea that Krasko had rented this villa outside of La Chorrera for him and Puii and Rune to live in; and had remodeled it to build a first-class laboratory for Puii; or that Puii had figured out how to take Khambang's seed tissue to the next level. Yes, it was *he*, Puii—Khambang's lowly assistant—and not Khambang, who had figured out how to grow the formative tissue—the final product! And in a few weeks, this final product would be ready to sell to Ravanco, for a new and much higher price, of course. Poor Khambang, Puii thought, he never had a clue.

Just then Puii's cell phone rang. He looked at the screen. It was Krasko.

*　*　*

A few minutes earlier, Krasko had been sitting in the VIP lounge of the Miami Executive Airport, a small private jet airstrip located on the outer edge of Miami, Florida. He was staring at this cell phone, just thinking. It was forty-five minutes ago when he had gotten that call from Violeta, one of his Bulgarian girls, saying that the three girls had been out shopping but were returning to the apartment in a taxi when they saw the police taking the two Colombian girls away in handcuffs. Violeta had been riding in the front seat. The two other girls—Ana and Svetla—always let Violeta sit in front because she was learning Spanish faster than they were. Violeta told the taxi driver in her basic Spanish to take them back to the mall they had just come from.

Krasko had congratulated her for thinking quickly, and told her to stay at the mall, and that he would call her back with instructions in exactly one hour.

Krasko liked Violeta. She was the smartest of the three. She could keep a cool head under pressure. Even if the police picked her up, she wouldn't tell them anything. The other two girls weren't as trustworthy, so Krasko and Violeta always kept them in the dark. Krasko only communicated with Violeta, and she told the other girls what to do. Yes, Krasko trusted Violeta. But still, he didn't want the police to pick her or the other two girls up.

When he had gotten her call, Krasko was in Miami

at Ravanco's office. He told his partners at Ravanco that he needed to get back to Panama ASAP. The Miami Executive Airport was just a thirty minute cab ride away from Ravanco's Miami office, and Ravanco kept a private corporate jet housed there just for its executives, and special VIP vendors like Krasko. They would fly him to the Dominican Republic, and from there he could catch a quick flight to Panama. Ravanco's office in the Dominican Republic was really just a shell subsidiary, used to provide a cover for moving people and product in and out of the United States. Ravanco provided Krasko with papers indicating that he was an employee working at their Dominican Republic office, which of course, wasn't true.

As he waited for the jet to be fueled up, he thought about what his next move would be. He thought it through and then dialed Puii's number through the encrypted WhatsApp service on his cell phone.

Puii was startled to see that Krasko was calling him. Krasko rarely did this. He answered the phone cautiously.

"Hello, Puii," said Krasko casually. "I need a favor. Would you go pick up our three friends and take them to a new hotel? They are not satisfied with their present accommodations. They saw a rat in the hallway, and it upset them."

"Of course," Puii said.

"You remember the store where we took them to buy clothes?" Krasko asked.

Puii remembered the fancy clothing store in the mall where he and Krasko had taken the girls the first day they arrived in La Chorrera and where Krasko had spent a lot of money buying them all new outfits.

"The fancy place? Yes, I remember it," Puii said.

"I'll have them meet you there. You should probably leave now and pick them up. And I think they need a change of scenery. Maybe book a nice hotel in a different town, somewhere quiet."

"Of course," Puii said. "I hope to see you soon."

"Yes, very soon. Goodbye."

And Krasko hung up. He looked at his watch. Exactly

one hour had passed from Violeta's call. He dialed her number, and she answered immediately.

"No worries, my darling," he said in Bulgarian. "You remember the fancy clothing store where we did all that shopping? Peter will pick you up there in a few minutes. Anything you need, you let him know."

Peter was the name that Krasko used for Puii when talking to Violeta, because she couldn't pronounce Puii.

Violeta said she understood, and hung up. Krasko sat and thought for a minute more. Hopefully, getting the girls out of La Chorrera would be a good thing. He would have to find out why the police arrested the two Colombians. It may be that he needed to dispose of them—he would decide that later.

Of course, Krasko didn't know that this was the *second* time that the police had taken the two Colombians in for questioning. The first time, the previous week, Jorge Manuel had released them after only two hours, and the two Colombians had agreed between themselves that they would not tell the blonde girls or the scary Bulgarian man about being arrested. If Krasko had known about that, things would have turned out differently. But he didn't know, and so things unfolded the way they did.

But being ignorant of the first arrest, Krasko tried to reassure himself that maybe this arrest had nothing to do with him. Maybe it was drugs or something minor like that. Besides, the Colombian girls really knew nothing. Still, he was worried. The fact that the police were sniffing around put a damper on his plans to get rid of Puii. He knew Puii had been communicating with someone in Karachi. After all, Krasko was the one who provided a laptop and cell phone to Puii when he brought him over to Panama. Was Puii so stupid as to not anticipate that Krasko would have bugs placed on both pieces of equipment? Evidently, he was. But now, worst case, he might have to move the laboratory out of La Chorrera. But hopefully not. The tissue was almost full-grown. If he could keep the police away for just a few more weeks, then he would be out of Panama for good. And by then, Krasko thought with a smile, he will have killed Puii and Rune.

The pilot came into the VIP lounge and told him that they were almost ready, and that he could board the plane in approximately ten minutes. Good, Krasko thought, he'd be in Panama before dark. He finished his drink and thought about the past week. He had stayed an extra week in Florida to meet with Ravanco officials to try and figure out a way to move the next shipment of tissue in one trip instead of six. But they thought it couldn't be done. There was just too much product, and it was too fragile. But they did say they would ask their engineers to try and build some special crates—maybe they could move it in three trips. That actually gave Krasko more options. He could schedule three deliveries, get paid for the first two, but then demand double for the final shipment. By then, he would have disposed of Puii and Rune. Or maybe he could sell the last shipment to China. So many options! In any event, then he could retire. He and his advisors at Mossack Fonseca had set up his retirement quite well. In two months, he would have almost half a billion dollars in ten different shell companies, with condos around the world for him to stay in, near beaches, and all the women and wine and cocaine he could want. Life would be good.

*   *   *

Puii hung up the phone. Okay, so Krasko was coming back. Good. He needed an infusion of cash. But why did he want the Bulgarian girls moved? And what did he mean when he said they saw a rat in the hall? Well, no matter... he would simply drive over to the mall and pick them up and take them somewhere. But where?

Puii opened a map. Krasko wanted them out of town. Probably a temporary measure. Puii looked at different options, and decided to look into the nearby town of Villa Rosario. It was much smaller than La Chorrera, probably a quiet place.

He got online and found the only upscale hotel in Villa Rosario—a place called Monteverde Vista—and made a reservation for a suite. He would drive over, pick up the whores and take them to Villa Rosario. He assumed that Krasko would bring them back to La Chorrera soon. He hoped Krasko would bring them back. He liked the sex parties they occasionally had at Krasko's villa; he especially liked fucking the younger Bulgarian girl, the one who never spoke.

*　*　*

And thus it came to pass, by the simple suggestion that he and Marco have lunch, that Ricardo set into motion a series of events... totally unbeknownst to him, that simply by suggesting, on the previous day, that Marco come to Villa Rosario the following day, the same day that Krasko called Puii, that Ricardo "caused" Marco to take the bus from La Chorrera to Villa Rosario, a bus that happened to pass by the front door of the Monteverde Vista Hotel in Villa Rosario, and that from his window seat on the bus, Marco would see Puii, whom he recognized as one of the Asian men that he had described to Jorge Manuel... he would see Puii escorting the three blonde Bulgarian girls up the steps to the Monteverde Vista Hotel... those same three girls that he also recognized, because he had often seen Krasko bring them to service guests at the Hotel de Cero, guests other than Khambang... Yes, Marco knew Krasco knew was pimping girls to other guests at his hotel. This was a fact that he had not revealed to Jorge Manuel that afternoon, some twelve days earlier, when the police chief was grilling him in the dead man's room. At the time, Marco felt he was already in enough trouble, and he didn't want to make his situation worse. Besides, Jorge Manuel hadn't asked. So Marco conveniently omitted the fact that Krasko had a regular business running those three blonde girls in and out of the Hotel de Cero. Sometimes Krasko would bring them, sometimes Puii would, but never Rune. Marco didn't know their names of course, but he knew their faces.

And perhaps "caused" is not the right verb to use... to say that Ricardo "caused" Marco to take that bus, that particular bus, that particular bus that happened to pass

91

by the Monteverde Vista Hotel… but what other verb would you use? Maybe you would say Ricardo "set into motion" or that he "precipitated a series of events"… but nonetheless… the events fell like dominoes (which, dear reader, is how Life falls… and Death, for that matter as well.) Yes, the events fell like dominos… Ricardo invited Marco to Villa Rosario; and Marco took the bus; and the bus passed by the Monteverde Vista Hotel just as Puii was escorting the three Bulgarian girls from a van up to the front door of the hotel; Marco saw this and recognized Puii and the three girls; and Puii did not see Marco; nor did the three girls see Marco….

And thus later, much later, after their lunch at El Balcón Restaurant, which of course Ricardo paid for, after Ricardo had suggested that Marco come back to Ricardo's apartment to hear some music, or have a glass of wine, or see some photographs, or whatever pretext it was that Ricardo had suggested, and after they both ended up in bed, and after they had had sex with each other… as they were lying together in Ricardo's bed, that the following conversation occurred:

"Ah…" said Marco, "so how was it you found me again?"

"I told you," Ricardo said. "Miguel told me you were working at that hotel."

"How did he know?"

"Oh, I don't know how he knew you worked there… you'd have to ask him that… but the name of the hotel came up because some policemen were having lunch at his restaurant a week or so ago, and they were discussing somebody who they thought had been killed at the hotel, and Miguel recognized the name of the hotel as the place where you worked."

Marco sat up in the bed. "What!?" he exclaimed.

"Oh relax, Marco," Ricardo said. "The cops weren't discussing you. They were simply discussing some case, and Miguel recognized the name of the hotel as the place where you worked."

"They said he was killed? Do they think it was a murder?" Marco asked with some alarm.

"No no no, well... I don't know," Ricardo said... "I mean, I wasn't there, I don't know what they think. Miguel just said... and understand Marco, this is just what he overheard, so he may have misheard... and you know how Miguel likes to gossip... but Miguel told me that the police seemed to be saying there was a murder of some guy at a hotel, and they named your hotel, and Miguel told me because he remembered that you worked at that hotel... that's all. And so when I was having lunch there yesterday, Miguel remembered all this and told me. No big deal."

Marco frowned and thought about it for a moment. The police never came back to talk with him. So he was not in any trouble. Still, he didn't like thinking about it. He slid back down into the bed and rubbed Ricardo's chest. "Well, I am glad Miguel mentioned my name to you, Ricardo. And I am glad that you took the effort to find me, but at the same time, I am concerned."

"Why?" Ricardo asked.

"Well... about two weeks ago, it's true, this guy died in one of our rooms. One of the housekeepers found him, and when the police showed up, they asked me a few questions, but when they asked me if I had told them everything I knew, well...I did not tell them everything."

At this point, a minute amount of adrenaline—just a micro-amount—was released in Ricardo's body. And while you would not have been able to observe it, this adrenaline was having an impact on Ricardo's brain. And even though they had just spent the last hour making love, an act of deep intimate sharing, an act so personal that you would think it would forgive a multitude of sins, Marco was now saying something that threatened to annul all that intimacy. Ricardo couldn't be sure. Was Marco saying that he had withheld something from the police about a murder case? Something important? Ricardo just wasn't clear what Marco meant... so he played dumb and said, "Marco, I have no idea what you mean. Start at the beginning and tell me."

And Marco, for his part, trusted Ricardo. Yes, it was true that Ricardo was a gringo, an older gringo, and it was true that some of Marco's friends had once teased him for being a protegido—or boytoy—of this old gringo, but Ricardo had always treated Marco decently; always paid his expenses; and never demanded any more sex than Marco expected to give for such kindnesses. Yes, Ricardo had always treated Marco with respect; always listened to Marco's problems; and always gave good advice; so that Marco, in fact, really trusted Ricardo, and thus it was that Marco told Ricardo everything that had happened at the Hotel de Cero regarding Khambang... and also those things he hadn't told the police....

"So, I answered all their questions, don Ricardo. But they never asked me if I had other encounters with these men. And the fact is... I saw them on other occasions... well, because when the hotel made me a manager, they said they would give me bonuses if I could increase the hotel occupancy rate. So I tried different things... but the only thing that worked was... well, you know, we get a lot of tourists at the hotel, many single men who come on vacation... turistas and Panamanian men who come to relax, maybe get away from their families, you know... and sometimes these men want women... well, I let those men—the gringo and the two Asians—I let them bring girls to the hotel for many guests. They had these three blonde girls... Panamanians love blonde women, you know... so I let them bring those blonde girls to the hotel for 'dates' with some of our guests. They would give me money to look the other way. And the hotel also paid me bonuses, because I rented more rooms. My shift usually runs from eleven in the morning to eight at night. The big gringo would text me when he was coming over, so I would be sure to be there. If they came after eight, I would tell the night clerk, Tomás, to let them in. Anyway, I didn't tell the police chief about that, because... well, because I didn't want to get into trouble."

"Uh huh," Ricardo said. "Well Marco, it may not be that important..."

"Well, first I thought so, too... because once the man died, you know, the big gringo stopped bringing the blonde girls to the hotel. So I figured that was the end of it..."

"It probably was, Marco... and besides, you just don't

know what happened."

"Well, it all seemed so weird, you know. The man dying, all that blood, and then you saying that the police think it was a murder... a murder in *my* hotel..."

"Well, Marco, that's only what Miguel thought he overheard them say..." Ricardo said, trying to reassure him. "I mean, I don't think it's anything to get upset about. It all seems to be over, to be in the past."

"Yes, except... I saw them today," Marco said.

"What do you mean?"

"I saw one of the Asian men taking the three blonde girls to the Monteverde Vista Hotel here in town."

"Really? Are you sure?" Ricardo asked.

"Oh yes, I recognized them. You know, you don't see a lot of blondes in Panama."

"True," Ricardo said. "So, maybe it's just a pimping organization that moves girls from hotel to hotel. It wouldn't be the first. It may have nothing to do with that guy dying."

Ricardo looked at Marco. He could tell that Marco was worried, so he said, "Look Marco, you can't get stressed over speculation. All you know is that some guy died in your hotel, right? That's the only fact you know. Everything else is speculation. There was nothing in the newspapers, right? Maybe Miguel misheard what your police chief and don Fernando were talking about. Maybe it wasn't a murder, but they were just speculating themselves—who knows? The police haven't come back to talk to you, right? I think you're getting worked up over nothing."

"Sí, you're probably right, Ricardo, but it is human nature to speculate and worry, is it not?"

Ricardo laughed, "Well, yes, that's true. It seems to be everyone's favorite occupation. But I tell you what. I know Dan Landes, the retired cop that was with don Fernando and your police chief at Los Cuñados. Why don't I talk with him and find out what the deal is?"

"Oh no, Ricardo," Marco said. "I do not want to get into any trouble."

"I'm not going to mention your name, Marco. But the next time I see him, I'll just chat with him and see if he'll talk about this case. After all, he owes me a favor... a big fucking favor."

"Okay, if you keep my name out of it, then yes, Ricardo, I would be very grateful if you would let me know."

"No problem, Marco."

The "big fucking favor" that Ricardo was referring to, of course, concerned that time a year or so ago, when the trajectory of Ricardo's life had previously intersected Dan's own orbit—and the orbits of don Fernando and Jorge Manuel as well—and I'm speaking, of course, of that case where that retarded blind muchacho had been murdered in that gay bathhouse in La Chorrera (a bathhouse that Ricardo and Miguel loved to visit); that case where Jorge Manuel felt overwhelmed, because the blind muchacho turned out to be the son of a wealthy and powerful family in La Chorrera; that case where Jorge Manuel had thus asked don Fernando for help, and where don Fernando in turn had dragged Dan over to La Chorrera; that case where Dan, who had no experience with gay bathhouses, had then enlisted Ricardo to help him, and had sent Ricardo into an S&M bathhouse in the city of Colón, almost two hours away, to flush out the killer. And of course, unbeknownst to Ricardo, that was also the same case where Dan witnessed the killer being, in turn, shot right in front of him, ten feet in front of him in fact, where Dan saw the side of the suspect's head being blown off—an experience that caused Dan to retreat back to the states for almost a year, before returning to Panama.

It's strange, isn't it, dear reader, how a single event can impact so many people in different ways? How each of us is in orbit around the same piece of ground, trying to maintain our flight, and then *Bam!* something happens that impacts us all—but impacts each of us differently—but our orbits and relationships are forever altered by such events, and the interesting thing is... that we rarely see how the same event shapes the lives of everyone around us. We simply only see how we are thrown off course, how we struggle to regain altitude, and how we manage to continue on as if we were the only one affected...

And thus in Ricardo's view, as he lay there in bed with Marco, a year or so after that murder case in the bathhouse, Ricardo only saw that Dan owed him a big favor, because that's what Dan had always claimed—and rightfully so—that he owed Ricardo "a big fucking favor" because, in fact, Ricardo had lured the killer out of that S&M bathhouse, so that Dan and don Fernando and Jorge Manuel could arrest the killer and solve the case. Ricardo simply had no idea that the killer had been murdered the next day, right in front of Dan... that in fact Ricardo's big favor had ended up being devastating to Dan, who had never witnessed a cold-blooded murder before... But, as said, that had been a year ago. Dan had retreated to the states to heal, and aside from his increasing dependence on ayahuasca, in many ways he had healed, and was able to return to Panama...

Yes, it is interesting how the invisible orbits of our lives intersect... because at that moment, as Ricardo was lying in bed with Marco, Dan was waking up from a long nap in his own bed... and neither Ricardo nor Dan had any idea that the orbits of their lives were about to collide again.

Chapter 8

*The other young man from Thailand
created the perfect double-cross plan,
but he had to move in a hurry
and he started to worry:
would this screw up his deal with Pakistan?*

As usual, Dan found it difficult to wake up. He always seemed to be climbing out of a steep, dark, muddy, slippery ditch, full of wet leaves that caused him to slide back into sleep, unless he struggled to wake up. If he could open at least one eye, see some light, determine if it was day or night, then he could force the rest of his body to continue climbing back to waking consciousness.

The light on the walls was yellow, and the shadows were long. He knew it was late in the day. He looked at the clock by the bed. It was almost 4:00 p.m. Jeez, he thought to himself, how long was I asleep? What day is it? His head felt foggy. He stretched his fingers, arched his shoulders, and wiggled his feet. Okay, he thought, at least all the parts are here—that's a start. Now, what day is it? He thought back. Oh yeah, yesterday he had gone with don Fernando to that lab in Panama City, and met that Dr. Vargas. She was rather attractive, Dan thought. He wondered if he could go see her again, maybe without don Fernando and Jorge Manuel. Perhaps on some unofficial police business... God, his head hurt. He moved his head from side to side, to stretch his neck. Why had he slept so long? Yesterday had been tiring, but still... And, if he had slept that long, why didn't he feel rested? He looked at his hands. They were trembling.

He reached down to the floor by the bed and found his plastic bottle of ayahuasca and looked at it. Plenty left. Oh well, he thought, and took a long sweet sip. The smoky liquid slid down his throat. Ahhh, so good. He placed the bottle back on the floor, and closed his eyes. He could taste the smoke all the way down. He could smell smoke... but it wasn't ayahuasca smoke...

He was back in the jungle, near the hut where he usually brewed the ayahuasca potion in the large iron cauldron. In the clearing next to the hut, he could see a ceremony of some kind. He looked, squinting his eyes. Men in pig masks were dancing around something that was burning... ah, it was some kind of pillory... oh... it was Khambang, still nailed upright to a bunch of planks that were wedged in the ground. Only this time, there were more sticks of wood piled around his feet, and smoke and flames were coming out... Oh shit, Dan thought, they're going to burn him at the stake...... Well, he *is* dead, but still...

Dan looked at the dancing men. They were short men, wearing nothing but loincloths and pig masks. They were each carrying spears and dancing around the staked body of Khambang. Dan looked closer at the dancers. Their bodies were odd: short, muscular but fat, completely hairless, fat bellies, short stubby legs... Dan blinked and strained his eyes. Wait... those weren't masks! Those were their faces! They all had faces like pigs: flattened pink noses, tiny beady eyes, pointed ears... They were pig men! And those weren't spears—they were AK-47s.

The phone was ringing. Dan turned and looked back to his hut. He needed some kind of a weapon, but he had none. He looked to the jungle. The phone was ringing. He started to run towards the jungle.

The phone was ringing. Groggily, instinctively, Dan reached over and answered it.

"What?" he mumbled.

"Dani? Dani, it's Fernando... Dani?"

"What is it, don Fernando?" Dan mumbled.

"Ah... are you okay, Dani?"

"I'm fine, don Fernando... call me tomorrow."

"Dani?" don Fernando said.

"No," Dan said, and hung up. Then he fell back to sleep.

This time he was flying... somewhere high in the clouds. Maybe he was a bird, he couldn't tell. Dan looked down and saw the city of Mumbai stretched out like a oozing festering sore of human misery, as far as the eye could see. Nothing but slum shanty shacks and windowless mega-factories. Slave labor, Dan thought. Under another name, but slave labor nonetheless. Born here in mud floor shacks, kept in poverty here, no schools here, bred only as labor to work in corporate factories that paid just enough pennies for the next meal.

Dan stretched his wings and made an arc to the right, angling towards one huge factory complex. What goes on in those factories, he wondered? What is being produced? Clothes for Westerners? Cheap computers? Knock-off purses? Cheap AK-47s? What's cheaper than guns, cheaper than bullets? Cost-to-benefit ratio, is there anything more politically effective than armaments?

He looked through the ceiling and walls of the factory and saw a line of homeless men, each receiving injections from Khambang and Puii, and then being escorted by Rune to rooms down a hall. Outside the factories, he saw the bodies of other homeless men being burned in huge bonfires. The stench and smoke from the fires burned his lungs. He pulled upward, aiming higher up, through the clouds.

*　*　*

Two days later, Jorge Manuel was sitting at his desk, thinking. He had done what Dan had suggested: he had had the two Colombian prostitutes re-arrested and kept in separate cells away from each other. He felt bad about having to make trumped-up charges to hold them, because he knew that they had done nothing illegal. But he had agreed with Dan that it was probably for the girls' own safety. He had brought them in, one by one, to the interrogation room and shown them pictures of the dead Khambang and showed them fake indictment papers he had drawn up, charging them with being accessories to murder. Both of the girls had cried and cried, and each had blubbered about how they were innocent, how they were just trying to make money to send to their families in Colombia.

The one thing that Jorge Manuel had noted was that each of the two girls told the exact same story. He and the sergeant had grilled each of them for hours, but every detail that each girl said was consistent with what the other girl said. So Jorge Manuel believed them. Krasko had initially only wanted a place to house the blonde girls. But when he discovered that the Colombians were trying to set up their own escort service, he offered to help them in exchange for them keeping an eye on the blonde girls, training them in Latino culture, and teaching them some Spanish. But it turned out that his "help" was only to pay them for sex parties—always at his villa or at that hotel when that third Asian man was in town once a month. Neither of the two Colombians liked the Bulgarian—he was scary—but he always paid them well.

After a day and a half of interviews, Jorge Manuel felt he had gotten all the information he could from the two Colombian girls. He called don Fernando and updated him on all that the girls had told him.

"So, where are the three blonde girls?" don Fernando asked.

"We don't know, don Fernando. They were not at the apartment when we arrested the Colombian girls. We have been looking for them for two days. We put the apartment under surveillance, but they have not returned. All their clothes are still there. We are hoping they just went somewhere on vacation and will return soon. As soon as they return, we will arrest them."

"Hmmm," don Fernando said. "Strange... Weren't there two other girls living at that apartment?"

"Sí, the two Brazilian prostitutes. They were not at home when we arrested the Colombians, either. But we saw when they came back. But after interrogating the Colombians, we decided not to arrest the Brazilian girls because they are not much involved," Jorge Manuel explained. "Evidently, the dead man preferred the two Colombian girls. And the Bulgarian and the two other Asians, well... they preferred to have sex with either the blonde girls, or the two Colombians as well. Evidently, no one wanted sex with the two Brazilian girls."

"I wonder why?" don Fernando said. Don Fernando was thinking of Giselle who, in fact, *was* from Brazil. Don Fernando actually liked Brazilian women the best. In experience, they were the best lovers. But, he thought, everyone has their own preferences.

"And how do you know the dead man didn't like the Brazilians?" don Fernando asked.

"Because the Bulgarian took the Brazilians over to the Hotel de Cero one time to have sex, and the dead man said he preferred the Colombians."

"Okay, and this big house they have... where the Bulgarian and the two Asians live, where is it?"

"In the country, outside of La Chorrera," Jorge Manuel said. "We had both Colombian girls draw us a map. We think we know where it is."

"Did the two Brazilian girls ever go there?" don Fernando asked.

"One time," Jorge Manuel said. "And that's where the Bulgarian and the two Asian men... well, I guess you would say, that's where they 'tried them out', but like I said, evidently those men preferred the other women as well."

"Uh huh... interesting," said don Fernando.

"So I was wondering, don Fernando, if you and I and your friend Señor Landes could get together again..." Jorge Manuel said optimistically.

"Well, Koke, I'm afraid Dani is a bit... indisposed. I talked to him for a few minutes two days ago, but I was not able to reach him all day yesterday. I am, in fact, on my way over to his house now to see if he is there. But I will tell you what I think, Koke. I think you should go over to the Colombia girls' apartment and arrest these two Brazilian girls as well. Then, can you draw up arrest warrants for these three men, and a search warrant for the house? I know we don't have enough to arrest any of them, but you can make something up. After I check on Dani, and you arrest those girls, I'll come to La Chorrera and get my brother-in-law to sign the papers. Then we'll go to this country house and arrest theses men. Dani thinks that we need to focus on the one Asian man he calls Puii. He thinks that we need to get this Puii guy to confess... but one thing at a time. You go to the girls' apartment and I'll go and try and find Dani."

"Okay, don Fernando... and thanks... thanks for all

your help on this case," Jorge Manuel said.

"Hey, Koke, no problem—we're family," don Fernando replied.

*   *   *

At this exact same moment, Krasko was walking through his villa's front door. He was just returning from an "errand."

"Puii!" Krasko called out.

"Here, boss," Puii answered.

"We need to move the lab," Krasko said as Puii entered the room.

"Move the lab? But...but why?"

"I went over to have a little chat with the cinnamon girls, but they are still in jail. But the other two girls were there. Remember them?"

Puii recalled the other two darker girls, both from Brazil. At one point, Krasko had taken them to Khambang at the Hotel de Cero. But Khambang preferred the lighter Colombians—the two "cinnamon girls." Puii had to agree with Khambang's taste. Both he and Krasko had fucked these two Brazilian whores as well, during a party in the villa, and both he and Krasko also preferred either the blonde girls or the two Colombian girls. Rune didn't seem to have a preference. He would have sex with whomever was left.

"Anyway," Krasko was explaining, "the police took our two favorite girls, but left these two Brazilians. But I had a little chat with these two... it was *very* interesting."

"How so?" Puii asked.

"Well, it turns out that this was the second time the police had arrested our two cinnamon girls. And the police already knew that they had had sex with Khambang *before* they arrested them the first time. Plus, those two cinnamon whores told the police that you and I and Rune would take them over to that hotel once a month."

Puii began to panic. "What?! When did this happen? When were they first arrested?" he exclaimed.

"More than a week ago," Krasko said. "But relax, Puii...

103

Those two cinnamon girls don't know anything more than that. And as you know—and as the police knew—paying them to have sex is not a crime. So they had to release them. But they told the two Brazilian girls, and made them both swear not to tell Violeta or Ana or Svetla It really pisses me off that those two cinnamon girls wanted to hide the fact that they had been arrested from me. That means they didn't trust me."

"What would you have done if they had told you?" Puii asked.

"Oh, I would have killed them, of course. But still, it bothers me that they didn't trust me."

"Why did they arrest them again?" Puii asked.

"That I do not know," said Krasko.

Puii thought for a minute. All of those girls had been to the villa at one time or another. Even if prostitution wasn't a crime, if the police came here, they would find the lab.

"Krasko, they all know this house!"

"I know, Puii," Krasko said, "That's why we have to move the lab today. Where did you say you parked Violeta and the girls?"

"In the Monteverde Vista Hotel in Villa Rosario. It's a little town about twenty-five minutes away."

"Okay, you and Rune start packing up the lab. I'm going to drive to Villa Rosario and rent a house. I'll be back as fast as I can. Have everything ready to move when I get back."

Krasko started to head back out the front door. Puii called out to him, "But Krasko, what about the two girls the police didn't arrest? Won't they tell the police they talked with you today?"

Krasko laughed and said over his shoulder, "Oh, I doubt it. They won't be talking to anyone... ever again."

* * *

"Dani, Dani, wake-up!" Don Fernando was shaking him. Dan opened his eyes. His room came into focus. He looked up at don Fernando, who was shaking him by the shoulders. The shaking made his head hurt even more.

"Stop shaking me!" Dan said. "I told you I didn't want to see you until tomorrow!"

"Dani," don Fernando said, letting go of his shoulders, "that was *two days ago*! I called you two days ago. I came over because you didn't answer your phone at all yesterday."

Dan looked around the room. The room looked normal. He looked at his hands. They seemed normal too—just a small trembling in the fingers. But his head hurt something awful.

"Oh, well in that case, don Fernando, come on in. Make yourself at home," Dan said. Then he looked at don Fernando and said, "You're kidding me, right?"

Don Fernando just shook his head no. Dan suddenly realized he was serious. Dan reached over to the side table and grabbed his cell phone. He looked at the date. It took him a few seconds to realize that he had been asleep... or had been something or somewhere... for days... in fact, it had been three days since he and don Fernando and Jorge Manuel were in Panama City visiting Dr. Vargas.

"Shit," was all he could say. He tried to think, but his head hurt too much. What had happened?

He pulled himself up on the bed and looked around the room again, and took a deep breath. He lifted the sheet up to see if he had peed in the bed. No, no sign of pee. He must have been sufficiently in control to at least get up and use the bathroom, he thought... but Jesus, three days? He looked up. Don Fernando was still standing there just looking at him.

"How did you get in here?" Dan asked.

"You gave me a key, remember? Before you left for the states last year. Told me to keep an eye on your landlord."

"Oh yeah," Dan said. "I had forgotten about that." Dan blinked a couple of times to try and figure this out. "Shit, don Fernando, I can't remember what happened. You brought me back here three days ago, right?"

"Sí, amigo," don Fernando said. "We got back late in the evening. You said you were tired and were going to go to bed... When I called you the next day, you seemed...

irritated… and told me to call you *yesterday…*"

"I'm sorry, don Fernando, I really am. I don't know what happened. I…I must have been drinking."

"Yes, Dani, you were drinking that devil's brew. It's going to kill you, you know. That stuff steals your soul; turns you into a zombie."

Dan thought for a moment. He *did* feel like a zombie.

"Yeah…" Dan didn't know what else to say.

Don Fernando took a deep breath and said, "Look, Dani, what if we get you into detox for a couple of days, just to clean you up, get you away from that stuff? I have a friend who…"

But Dan interrupted him. "Well, I tell you what, don Fernando, right now what I really need is food… food and coffee… why don't I take a quick shower and we go out to eat, and we can talk about this over some breakfast? Okay?"

Don Fernando looked at his friend, sighed, but nodded his head. "Okay, Dani… okay, I'll wait outside."

Don Fernando went outside to wait. Dan took a quick shower, then got dressed. He filled his flask with ayahuasca and stuck it in his pocket. Then he took a long swig from the plastic bottle before he went outside to don Fernando's car.

*   *   *

"God, I am starved," Dan was saying as he bit into his breakfast of scrambled eggs, sausage, and rice and beans at the Mariscos restaurant. "This food is great, don Fernando. Are you sure you don't want anything to eat?"

"No, Dani, I ate breakfast several hours ago," don Fernando said dryly.

"Well, I feel like I haven't eaten in days," Dan said and smiled broadly at don Fernando. He said this, of course, simply to irritate his friend. But the fact was, he felt better. His headache was gone, and even though he still couldn't remember much about the visions he had, he felt that his thinking was clear.

"So what's new on our piggy case?" Dan asked.

Don Fernando winced at that glib moniker, but said,

"Well, you were right about that blood-soaked cloth—it matched the DNA in the tissue that Dr. Vargas scraped from that ice chest."

"Yeah, I figured," Dan said between bites. "It doesn't make any difference, but here's the deal: This Khambang dude needed human DNA to make his stuff... well... let's just call this tissue his piggy stuff. It didn't really matter whose DNA it was, but he needed human DNA. Originally, when he set up his laboratory in Mumbai, they just killed people in the neighborhood and used their DNA to make the tissue. But once Khambang perfected the process, they just needed a tiny bit of DNA to create the stem cells, so he—being an egotistical idiot—used his own DNA. By that time, they had the process down... and so he grows this piggy stuff in some laboratory in Mumbai, and then he brings it here, and then this Krasko guy buys it from him and delivers it to Ravanco in the states."

"How do you know this?" don Fernando exclaimed, exasperated.

Dan took another bite of rice and beans. "Oh, I saw it in my visions," he said.

Don Fernando just closed his eyes and shook his head. He thought of poor Jorge Manuel trying to write an affidavit for a search warrant. "Well, your honor, this drugged-out ex-cop had a vision where he saw this and that..."

Dan sensed don Fernando's frustration and said: "Look, don Fernando, I know you don't approve of my taking ayahuasca... and I know it takes a toll on my body... but it enables me to...to see certain things."

Don Fernando opened his eyes and looked at Dan. This was the first time that Dan voluntarily talked about ayahuasca. This could be don Fernando's opportunity.

"I know, Dani, but I have seen too many people die from using it."

"Really?" Dan asked. "Like who?"

"You don't know them. But for example, I had a friend named Oscar Hernandez who drank ayahuasca and he ended up committing suicide."

"Oscar Hernandez committed suicide because his

wife left him, not because he drank ayahuasca," Dan said.

Don Fernando stared at Dan. "Wait... you didn't know him. He died fifteen years ago, long before you came to Panama."

"True, don Fernando, true..." Dan said, staring coldly at don Fernando. "But I am connected to anyone who is a devotee of ayahuasca, whether I have ever met them or not. I see beyond time." Dan smiled and took another bite of food.

A shiver ran through don Fernando. For a moment, he was not sure if the man in front of him was his friend of ten years or some brujo who had taken over his friend's body.

Dan looked up and smiled again. "Relax, my friend, relax, and tell me what else has happened with our piggy case."

Don Fernando took a deep breath and tried to relax. It occurred to him that he had been assuming that Dani was either crazy or right, but maybe it was both: Maybe Dani was crazy *and* right.

So he exhaled slowly and told Dan about how Jorge Manuel had arrested the two Colombian girls, but how the three blonde girls had gotten away; about Jorge Manuel's questioning of the two Colombian girls; about the existence of Krasko's villa; and about the fact that at that moment Jorge Manuel was on his way to arrest the two Brazilian girls.

"You mean," Dan asked, "he didn't arrest the Brazilians when he arrested the Colombians?"

"No, when the police converged on the apartment, the only ones there were the Colombians. He put the apartment under surveillance and saw when the two Brazilian prostitutes came back, but he hasn't arrested them yet. But he'll do that today."

"Hmmm," said Dan. He put his fork down, leaned his head back, and closed his eyes.

"And after he does that," don Fernando continued, "then I will go to La Chorrera and talk with my brother-in-law. Then we will get arrest warrants and search warrants and go to this villa of the Bulgarian man and arrest everyone there. I am betting that the blonde girls are there too."

"Hmmm," said Dan again. "Hmmm."

Just then don Fernando's cell phone rang.

"Hola," don Fernando answered. "Ah, Koke, dígame."

And then don Fernando's face lost color.

"Okay, Koke. Okay, let me call you right back."

Don Fernando hung up.

Dan opened his eyes and said, "Let me guess. The two Brazilian girls are dead."

"Sí, amigo. They had their throats slit."

"Okay, I tell you what, don Fernando. Call Jorge Manuel back. Tell him we'll be there in thirty minutes. As soon as we get there, we'll all just go to this villa out in the country and see what's there."

"But we'll need the search warrants first, Dani."

"Mmmmm... no we don't. We can claim exigent circumstances," Dan said, waving to the waiter for the bill.

"What does 'exigent circumstances' mean?" don Fernando asked.

"It means we can do what we want," Dan replied.

Chapter 9

There was an ex-cop from the states...

Jorge Manuel had the two hand-drawn maps from the two Colombian girls, but the back roads in Panama are, shall we say, not well marked, and the maps were the best that the two girls could remember... but not so accurate. So it took Jorge Manuel, don Fernando, Dan, and the other police almost three hours to find Krasko's villa. Fortunately, both girls' description of the actual house was good. They both said it was an "amarillo brillante" color—bright yellow. So don Fernando and Jorge Manuel would stop every few miles or so, and get out to ask different farmers and field workers where there might be a large bright yellow house, and each time they left the car, Dan would discretely take a little swig from his flask. Through the process of trial and error, the police eventually finally found the villa.

When the three police cars had pulled up in front of the yellow house, both Jorge Manuel and don Fernando looked at Dan.

"Okay, Dani," said don Fernando, "we don't have an arrest warrant or a search warrant. How exactly does this 'exigent circumstances' method work?"

Dan laughed, "Ah, we just go up and knock."

"And then what?"

"Well, then we break the door down," he laughed again. "Come on, this will be fun."

Don Fernando just shook his head and followed Dan out of the car. Dan stood there a minute and looked at the house. There were no cars in the driveway, and no signs of activity.

"Besides, don Fernando," Dan said, "I have the sense

that no one is home."

Dan walked up to the front door. Jorge Manuel told the sergeant to have his men spread out behind Dan and to be watchful. Jorge Manuel knew that Dan wasn't carrying a gun.

Dan knocked loudly on the door, but there was no answer. Don Fernando kept his hand on his revolver. Dan tried the front door handle. It was unlocked. He opened the door wide. He was about to step in when don Fernando grabbed his shoulder and stepped in front of him, his gun drawn, and shouted, "Policía! Policía!" Dan and Jorge Manuel and two other policemen followed him inside. The sergeant sent several men around the sides of the building.

*   *   *

At that same exact moment, Krasko, Puii, and Rune were on the outskirts of Villa Rosario, moving the large glass incubators into the rustic farmhouse that Krasko had rented.

"It isn't as nice as the villa in La Chorrera," Krasko explained to Puii and Rune, "but it was available immediately. The owner lives in town now, and he has been trying to sell it for two years, but hasn't had a single offer. I offered to rent it for a month and told him that if I liked, I would buy it. He liked my cash, that's for sure. The tissue will be ready in a month, right Puii?"

"Three weeks, tops," said Puii, looking around the farmhouse. "Does this place have air-conditioning?" he asked.

"I thought the tissue didn't need air-conditioning," Krasko said.

"It doesn't," Puii replied, "but I like it. It's hot in here."

"Open a window," Krasko said gruffly.

Krasko looked around. "No, this place suits me. It's outside of town, no neighbors, and it reminds me of the old country—simple construction." He pointed to a door at the end of the hallway. "Take a look at that bedroom there—I thought that would be a good incubation room."

Puii walked down the hall and looked in the room. Actually it would be a perfect incubation room, he thought—

dark and humid. He walked back out to the front room.

"Yes, that will do nicely, Krasko," he said. "Rune, let's move the incubators into that room."

Rune nodded and started to pick up one of the glass aquariums that Puii had modified into an incubator.

"And don't drop another one!" Krasko barked out and glared at Rune.

Rune nodded meekly and carried the incubator carefully. He had dropped one of the incubators at the villa in La Chorrera when he and Puii were rushing to get everything packed up before Krasko got back from house-hunting. The glass had broken into several large pieces. Luckily, Puii had an extra incubator and was able to save the tissue. Krasko was furious when he found out, but Puii reassured him that no tissue had been lost in the accident.

Puii went out to the Krasko's van and brought in two suitcases. Maybe he could buy a window air-conditioner in town for his bedroom. He missed the big yellow house in La Chorrera already—it was luxurious. He wondered if Villa Rosario even sold air-conditioners in town. When they had driven through the village on their way here, it looked pretty small and simple. He saw a mercado, a few restaurants, and a hardware store—maybe the hardware store sold air-conditioners—and there was also, of course, a large Catholic Church. He didn't see a liquor store, but he assumed there would be one somewhere. He wondered if Krasko would still continue to bring the Bulgarian girls over to this place for their twice-a-week sex parties. Or maybe they would all go to the Monteverde Vista Hotel for those events. He knew the hotel would have air-conditioning. Either way, there would be sex. Krasko had to have his sex. Plus, it had been part of the deal for enticing Puii into this project—not only had Krasko promised him lots of money and a decent laboratory for his work, but he had included the services of prostitutes... twice a week... Both he and Krasko had gotten used to that schedule back in Thailand. Originally Krasko wasn't going to let Rune have access to any of the hookers, but Puii insisted that Rune have some too. After all, Puii knew firsthand how problematic a disgruntled employee could be, so he was not going to give Rune any excuse for betraying him the same way that Puii had betrayed Khambang. So he had insisted from the start that Rune share in the orgies. Krasko agreed, reluctantly, but only gave Rune whatever hooker was left over after Krasko and Puii made their choices. When Krasko brought the two Colombians over for sex, Rune had to wait until either Krasko or Puii was finished before he could have his turn. But Puii knew that Rune didn't mind—Rune was neither handsome nor confident, so he was just grateful for any sex whatsoever.

*   *   *

"I didn't think anyone would be here," Dan was explaining to don Fernando, "because there were no cars out front." Dan was bending down examining the broken aquarium glass in one of the back rooms.

The police had searched the Villa and found no one. Now they were searching through drawers looking for any type of document that might identify the recent occupants. Dan was squatting down on his haunches and using a pen to move the different pieces of glass aside on the floor and examine them.

"Jorge Manuel," he called out.

"Sí, Señor Landes," Jorge Manuel.

"Do you have an evidence technician here?" Dan asked.

"Sí," and Jorge Manuel called Andrés over to where Dan was kneeling, examining the broken glass. "This is Andrés," Jorge Manuel said.

"Andrés," Dan said, "do you have any sterile containers of any kind?"

Andrés shook his head no.

"Okay then," said Dan, "Well, you see these pieces of broken glass? Can you gather them carefully and place them in some kind of container—not a bag, but a box of some kind."

"Sí, señor," Andrés said.

"Good," said Dan, "And, do you have an extra pair of latex gloves?"

113

Andrés nodded and handed Dan a pair of gloves. Dan put them on and picked up a piece of glass, approximately the size of a large coin. He brought it close to his eyes and looked at it. Then he held it up to Andrés to look at. "You see how there is something smeared on the glass? I don't want to lose this stuff, whatever it is. See if you can place any piece of glass with something smeared on it face-up in the box, so that this stuff doesn't get squished. And then give me the box."

Don Fernando and Jorge Manuel came over to where Dan was squatting.

"What is it?" Jorge Manuel asked.

"I don't know," Dan said, "But I'm hoping it's more of that tissue. Something broke here, and they tried to sweep it up. Over in the trash can there you'll see the frame of some type of glass box, like an aquarium, but there's no water on the floor. That reminds me—Andrés?"

"Sí, señor?"

"Let's take that trash can back to the police station and dust the frame for prints. And that broom handle... also, any pieces of glass that might be in the trash can too, unless they have any of this gray stuff on them, in which case, put them in the box for me."

Dan stood up. "I want to take this glass back to Dr. Vargas and have her take a look at it. Did you all find anything?"

"Not yet," Jorge Manuel said.

While Andrés was carefully collecting the broken pieces of glass, Dan and the two police chiefs inspected the villa. They walked through the back room where there were test tubs and jars of various chemicals. Shelves were built into two of the walls.

"I'm guessing this was their laboratory," Dan said.

They walked through the rest of the villa. Dan noted the dishes piled high in the sink, the rumpled bed sheets, the towels on the floor in the bathroom, and the empty closets.

"These guys cleared out of here fast," he said to Jorge Manuel. "They took all their clothes and personal belongings but left the sheets, blankets, and towels... so obviously this place must be rented as a furnished house... which means, they rented it from someone. We need to find out who the owner is and see if he has any information about these guys, their full names, maybe a passport number... but I suspect we won't find much. I'll bet the owner doesn't even know they're gone."

Andrés walked up to Dan holding a clear rectangular plastic box with the broken glass inside.

"Here are all the pieces with something on them," he said to Dan.

Dan took the box. "Thanks, Andrés, and can you do me one more favor? Can you look at the dishes and silverware in the sink? I think we should preserve anything that might have fingerprints on it... it might be another link of evidence we can use... and I guess that would include any of these guys' DNA that might be on the forks and spoons. You never know. And check the sheets and pillows for hair samples and DNA too. Shit, you're going to need a truck to haul this stuff out of here."

Dan turned toward Jorge Manuel and asked, "Can you call Dr. Vargas and see if she's available today?"

Then he asked don Fernando, "Can I borrow one of your patrol cars?"

"What?" asked don Fernando.

"Can I borrow one of your patrol cars? If Dr. Vargas is available, I want to drive to Panama City and take this glass to her."

"We'll go with you," don Fernando exclaimed.

"No, I want to talk with her alone," Dan said.

Don Fernando paused. This confused him. "But Dani, we are not allowed to let civilians drive the patrol cars."

"Exigent circumstances," Dan said and smiled.

"Uh, no Dani... look, I can have one of my officers drive you," don Fernando offered.

Dan gave a big dramatic sigh and rolled his eyes, mostly to tease his friend, and said, "Oh *okay!* don Fernando, get someone to drive me, but he has to stay in the car while I meet with Dr. Vargas."

Don Fernando nodded, although he was still confused why Dan didn't want him or Jorge Manuel along for the ride.

Jorge Manuel hung up his cell phone and said to Dan, "She can meet you at the lab in an hour."

Don Fernando motioned to one of the officers and told him to drive Dan to Panama City.

"Thanks, amigo," Dan said cheerfully to don Fernando as he left with the officer.

After Dan left, Jorge Manuel and don Fernando talked.

"He didn't want us to go with him?" Jorge Manuel asked.

"Apparently not... most definitely not," don Fernando replied. "But I don't know why. He just said he wanted to talk to her alone."

"Well," Jorge Manuel said, "She *is* pretty."

"True," don Fernando said, "but I don't know if that was his reason. I worry about him, Koko. He's been acting strangely. He...well, he drinks a lot."

Jorge Manuel nodded his head but said, "He seemed normal to me."

"Yeah," don Fernando said. He thought about confiding Dan's ayahuasca habit to his nephew, but decided there was no point in doing so. "Well, Koko, let's finish up here and see if we can track down the owner of this building."

Chapter 10

*There was an ex-cop from the states
who was good at tempting the fates...*

"I brought you a present," Dan said to Dr. Vargas when she came down to the lobby to greet him. "Is there somewhere we could talk?"

Dr. Vargas looked at the plastic box that Dan was holding, frowned, but said, "Yes, of course, come with me."

She told the guard that Dan was there on official business. She took him up the elevator to the fifth floor, and they went into the same conference room that they had been in before. Dan placed the plastic box on the table. Dr. Vargas peered through the plastic sides of the box at the pieces of broken glass, but she did not open the box.

"What did you bring?" she asked as they sat down.

"I'm not sure exactly what it is, but it's related to the tissue smear that was on the ice chest... only...only, this is different," Dan said. "The tissue in the ice chest was a reddish color when it was brought into this country, and it was thin, runny. When these people brought it in through the airport, it was in these plastic sheets with bubbles—pockets—like a plastic ice tray sealed at the top, with each pocket holding a tablespoon of the tissue. One of the pockets had split open and that's why a bit of the tissue had gotten smeared on the side of the ice chest. But this stuff," he said gesturing to the plastic box, "came from a small aquarium tank. It had broken... I suspect someone dropped it, and the glass had shattered. We found the frame of the aquarium in a trash can along with the broken glass. But some of the glass had this gray matter stuck to the side, and that's what I brought you. Like I say, this stuff is different—it's gray and thicker than the red tissue—but I know it's related somehow."

"The glass from this 'aquarium'—is it thick or thin?" Dr. Vargas asked, still peering at the plastic box.

"Thick," Dan said.

"It might be an incubator of some type," she said.

Dan closed his eyes. Of course, he thought to himself. Of course. You have to *raise* children... Khambang's children. You have to grow tissue.

"I think that's exactly what it was," he said, opening his eyes.

"Well, we can analyze the tissue, analyze the DNA," Dr. Vargas said, "and then we'll know if it's related to the earlier sample."

"I want you to do more than that, Doctor," Dan said. "I want you to *grow* it."

Dr Vargas' mouth opened, then closed, then she said quietly, "What?"

"I want you to grow this tissue. We have to see what the final product is," Dan said.

Dr. Vargas looked at the plastic box and then back at Dan.

"But...but this may be human DNA tissue..." she said.

"Oh, I *know* it is," Dan replied.

"Señor Landes, if there is human embryonic tissue in here, and if I were to 'grow it' as you say... if that even could be done... I would be committing an ethical violation in my profession. I simply cannot do that."

"I know you're not allowed to," Dan said, "but these are exigent circumstances."

"What?"

"Let me explain, Doctor. The last time I was here I told you that this was a murder case. But that's just how we got involved. This is a much, much bigger case than that. This is an international crime that affects many countries... I don't even know how to begin... Look, people are being murdered over this tissue, three people in Panama already... because there is some final product that this tissue produces that makes it very valuable, not to individuals, but to governments..."

Dan stared out the window for a moment, closed his eyes, took a deep breath, opened his eyes, and began, "We're still missing a lot of the pieces, and a lot of it doesn't make sense yet, but let me tell you what we know: there is this international company, based in the United States—we don't know much about them except they have lots of money—and they are the ones who were funding the development of this tissue in Thailand. And it was illegal in Thailand, but they were paying off all these legislators and scientists, but they got caught. So they moved their operation to Mumbai, India, where they built a giant factory of some kind to figure out how to grow this tissue... But they needed humans to experiment on—I don't know why. Initially, they were taking these poor people in Mumbai and experimenting on their bodies... using their bodies to grow tissue, or seeing what the tissue did to their bodies, I don't know... But finally at some point they perfected their process on whatever it was that they were trying to grow, and they just needed a bit of human DNA because now they had this stuff they could grow in lab—this red tissue—being produced in Mumbai. But they need to get it to the United States. So they were smuggling it in through Panama. Now, whatever this stuff is, it's not legal, which is why they have to smuggle it into the United States. Well, the courier who brought it in, he was the one who developed it, but he was murdered. That's whose blood was on that cloth, and that's whose DNA you found in the tissue in the ice chest. Anyway, this courier was murdered by these three guys, who are somewhere here in Panama. One's from Bulgaria and the other two are from Thailand. And the FBI knows about this, because as soon as this guy got murdered, they flew to Panama and stole his body and took it back to the United States. And there were two women who knew these three guys who murdered the courier, and they've been murdered, too. Oh, and when we sent the ice chest to the FBI's DNA lab to analyze, they claimed it was just pig blood, nothing more. But then, like I said, they showed up the next day and stole the dead man's body...

Dr. Vargas was looking at Dan with her mouth open.

He paused, searching for words, then said: "I know that sounds like a fantastic story... but is it any more fantastic than what you found? Rings of pig DNA spliced into human DNA? Some kind of technology that no one else has? Well, think about it—it was done for a purpose. This tissue was man-made for a purpose. It's supposed to grow into something, or produce something, or... lead to something... something so valuable that people are being murdered for it. We have to find out what that final product is, what that purpose is."

Dr. Vargas stared at Dan. "Is all you are telling me, is it true?" she asked.

"Yes, you can talk with Jorge Manuel or don Fernando and they will confirm everything that I have told you."

"And do you have any idea what the 'final product' of this tissue is, Señor Landes?" she asked.

Dan looked down at the floor. "I have a fear of what it might be."

"And what is that?"

"Well, you know how chimera is named after a Greek myth—the three headed creature made up of different animals?"

"Yes."

"Well, there's another Greek myth—the story of Saturn, otherwise known as Moloch, that eats its own children. I think this tissue is more than just modified human DNA. It's modified to attack other tissue, to ingest it and convert it into something else. That's why your technicians thought it was attacking pig cells... because that's exactly what it was doing. It's a combination of DNA and some mechanism—maybe some virus, or something... I don't know—but something that converts..." Dan took a breath. "That converts animals into something else, something half-human... I'm not sure what."

Dr. Vargas looked at the plastic box again, then said, "It is against the ethical rules for me to grow human life in a lab, Señor Landes, but I will study this tissue. Maybe I can run some mathematical models that will tell me what it is designed to do. This may take several days. But I will consider what you have told me."

Dan nodded. "That's fair doctor. Feel free to talk with Jorge Manuel and don Fernando about what I have told you. But I would caution you about talking to anyone else about it. Trust no one. Keep this tissue safe."

Dan scribbled out his phone number on a piece of paper. "Do what you can. Here's my phone number. Call me if you can figure out what this stuff does, and ... and thank you."

Dr. Vargas nodded.

Dan stood up. He felt oddly exhausted. He just wanted to sleep. He thanked her again and walked out of the room.

When he got out of the building and climbed back into passenger seat of the patrol car, the police officer who had driven him there told him that Jorge Manuel had instructed him to drive Dan back to Villa Rosario if Dan wanted.

"Yes, that would be nice," Dan said.

Dan looked at his hands. They were shaking. He reached into his pocket and felt his flask. But he decided against taking a sip. Maybe don Fernando was right. Maybe he needed to taper off the stuff a little bit. He leaned his seat back and closed his eyes.

*   *   *

Just about the time that Dan was drifting off to sleep in the patrol car, Ricardo and Miguel were easing themselves into the large hot tub at the gay bathhouse in La Chorrera.

"Ahhh, the water, it is so good. I have been on my feet all day," Miguel was saying.

Ricardo was adjusting the jets so they hit the small of his back.

"Yes, Miguel, we are lucky to have this place," he said.

"Speaking of lucky," Miguel asked, "were you able to hook up with young Marco?"

"Yes... yes, I was. He came and had lunch with me in Villa Rosario two days ago. It was good to see him. Thank you again for telling me where he worked."

"Ah, I am glad that worked out, my friend," said Miguel. "There is nothing quite like love. It makes the world go round, especially for old gray foxes like ourselves."

"I think the expression in English is silver fox, not gray fox," Ricardo said.

"Really? I must remember that. I'm always trying to improve my English, you know. We get more and more gringo customers in the restaurant these days, and none of them speak any Spanish. You know, when you first moved here, what? ten? eleven? twelve? years ago? ... remember? You were one of the only gringos who came to my restaurant. Nowadays, I always have more gringos than Panameños."

"Really? Well, that's a good thing, isn't it?"

"Oh yes, much better for business. In the first place, the waiters are much happier, because gringos always tip well. Even though the tip is added onto the bill, they still leave a tip *after* paying the bill. It's crazy! When the register prints out their bill, it clearly says at the bottom 'ten percent service charge included' but they can't read Spanish!" Miguel laughed. "Makes the waiters very happy."

"I bet," Ricardo said.

"And in the second place, I no longer have to put the gringo tables in the back room because they are so loud. If all the tables are gringos, they can be as loud as they want."

"True," Ricardo said.

"The only thing though," Miguel said with a frown, "is that some of your countrymen are very rude. You know, most of our waiters understand English, and they hear the gringos say such terrible things about our culture, about Panameños, about our women... they say the men are all lazy and the women are all whores! It makes the waiters very angry. They work very hard and their wives are good women."

Ricardo shook his head. "I know, Miguel. It's horrible. I've said this before, but it's *embarrassing* when I see gringos act that way."

"But you are a gringo and you do not act that way," Miguel said. "Why do they?"

"I don't know, Miguel... maybe it's genetics. Remember, my mother was Spanish. So even though I was born in the states, I have different blood."

"Does that make a difference, amigo?" Miguel asked.

"Well," Ricardo explained, "remember that when the U.S. was colonized by England, they kind of used it as a place to dump all their prisoners. For example, the state of Georgia was founded as a penal colony—the entire state! And of course there was a lot of inbreeding, so even after 300 years, a lot of those same genetic tendencies are still around, you know, stupid criminal genes and stuff. That's why they have a higher crime rate in Georgia than the national average... and things like the most lynchings of any state in the U.S."

"Ha! I did not know that about Georgia. A penal colony, huh? Did they build a big wall around the state to keep the prisoners in?"

"They didn't have to, Miguel. Where could the prisoners run to? South Carolina? No, the whole point was simply to get those prisoners out of England... send them to the U.S. colonies or to Australia... Cull the herd, so to speak. That's why the British are so damn polite, you know. They've simply exiled all their aggressive genes... Ha!"

Miguel laughed too. "Is that really true about Georgia?" he asked.

"Yeah, actually it is. England sent convicts to Virginia and Maryland too. Anywhere they could dump their refuse. In fact, in some parts of West Virginia, up in the hills, they still speak with a British accent, even after 300 years."

"Really?" exclaimed Miguel.

"Uh huh. That's just how long those traits stay in a culture... Assuming that stupidity and racism are inheritable traits, which I think they are... but even assuming they're not, the culture of stupidity and racism gets passed along to each new generation. So I'm afraid as long as there are gringo tourists, they will continue to say rude things within earshot of your waiters. You just need to explain to your waiters that gringos are really just exiled criminals."

"Well, I just tell the waiters to not take it personally, that the gringos simply are ignorant and don't know," Miguel said.

"They don't *want* to know," Ricardo countered. "They want to stay ignorant. Like I say, it's embarrassing. It makes me ashamed to be an American."

"Well, amigo, your country *is* strange," Miguel said, "so very violent lately, too. It's crazy."

"Oh Miguel, I know. I don't even read the news anymore. It just makes me so sad; it's like all common sense has gone out the window. The rhetoric and posturing and threats just keep worse and worse. It's like a contest where everyone is trying to be the most provocative, the biggest bully."

Miguel nodded his head in agreement.

Then Ricardo added quietly, "It's like the world has gone insane. At times, Miguel, I worry another world war is coming."

Miguel looked at Ricardo. "Seriously? Between whom?"

"Oh, it doesn't matter," Ricardo said. "Something will happen… somebody will cross some line… and countries will choose up sides. It won't matter who sides with whom… But the way things are escalating… eventually they have to blow… like a volcano."

"Ah amigo, I hope not," Miguel said.

"Yeah, me too… This is why I don't like to talk politics," Ricardo said. "It just makes me crazy to think about it."

Miguel smiled. "Nor do I. What say we wander into the steam room and see what trouble we can get into?"

"Now you're talking," Ricardo said.

And both men climbed out of the hot tub.

*   *   *

The next morning, don Fernando was sitting in his office, wondering where he might have lunch, when Jorge Manuel called.

"Uncle, I sent a fax to the FBI, like Señor Landes suggested, complaining that they had taken all my evidence—the body of the dead man and the ice chest—and you won't believe what they faxed back."

"Tell me, Koko."

"Well, they claimed the dead was a U.S. citizen, and that they did an autopsy and that he died of natural causes!"

"What?! No!" exclaimed don Fernando.

"Sí. I couldn't believe it. I took the fax over to Thai embassy. At first, the consulado said he couldn't talk with me, but when I told him what the FBI had said, he got mad again, and brought me into his office. I showed him the fax, and he said there was no way, that the dead man had never been a U.S. citizen, that he had never even been to the United States, that his parents were Thai and that he was born in Thailand. He swore up and down that the FBI was lying. And then he—I think because he was so mad—he told me that after I had visited him the first time, he got a call from something called the Armed Forces Security Center in Thailand telling him to stay out of this whole matter, that they had their own agents working on this case."

"What?" exclaimed don Fernando. "Why?"

"Well, that's what made him so mad, uncle. Evidently, the embassies in Thailand are supposed to be independent... well, independent of the military anyway. They report to the Prime Minister. They're not supposed to be taking orders from the military. But here was the military giving him orders. So he called his bosses in Thailand and they didn't know a thing about this, but told him to not talk to me until they could figure it out."

"Weird," said don Fernando.

"You know, uncle, I rather liked this consulado guy. He seems to take his job seriously. He said he'd been working in their embassies all his life, always trying to help Thai citizens around the world. He told me that there has been this tension in Thailand between the military and the government since the early sixties, because of what happened in Burma, next door to them, when the military took over the government. Anyway, he was very nice, but told me he still couldn't talk to me anymore, but that he would call me once his bosses in Thailand told him it was okay."

Don Fernando thought for a minute, then asked: "And

tell me again what the FBI said about doing an autopsy?”

“They said they had done an autopsy and determined that this Khambang guy had died of natural causes.”

“But didn’t your Dr. Espinoza already do an autopsy?”

“Sí, uncle, he did.”

Don Fernando was exasperated. “Well, Koke, wouldn’t it be obvious that the body had already had an autopsy done?! Wouldn’t it be cut open?”

“I *know*, uncle. It just makes no sense. Either they’re stupid or they think we’re stupid.”

“Okay, I tell you what, Koke,” don Fernando said. “Fax the FBI back, thanking them for their fax. Be very polite. Don’t contradict them. In fact, tell them you are satisfied with their response and that you are closing the case.”

“What?”

“Well, you see, I agree with you,” don Fernando explained. “Either they are very stupid or they think we are. So let’s let them be content either way.”

At that moment, don Fernando looked up and saw Dan standing in his doorway, waiting patiently. He had not heard him come down the hallway.

“Ah... Koke, can I call you back?”

“Of course, uncle.”

Don Fernando hung up the phone and looked at his friend. Dan looked haggard and pale.

“Come in, Dani, come in,” don Fernando said, pointing to a padded chair next to the desk.

Dan seemed to stumble a bit as he walked over to the chair. He turned the chair to face don Fernando, and sat down. Dan pursed his lips, looked at his hands, and then at his friend.

“Don Fernando, I need some help,” he said softly.

Chapter 11

"What's wrong, Dani?" don Fernando asked.

Dan shrugged his shoulders, and shook his head. "Well, okay" he began, "I'm having a problem..." He looked around the room, then said, "Yesterday, you know, I went to see Dr. Vargas, and last night, when I got back, I didn't feel well, but I...I told myself I wasn't going to drink ayahuasca... because... I don't know... maybe just to prove to myself I could go one night without it..." He shook his head. "I couldn't do it, don Fernando. I got the shakes so bad... I hurt so bad... I saw... *terrible* things... that finally I had to drink it just so I could get some sleep... Then this morning, I had to drink it again, just to wake up."

Don Fernando nodded his head. He had, unfortunately, seen this before.

"You are poisoned, Dani, that's all," don Fernando said. "You have drank too much of that devil drink."

"I feel okay now... I mean, not okay, but... normal enough," Dan said, "but I know that in a couple of hours, if I don't drink some more, I'll start shaking again, and seeing bad things again..." His voice trailed off.

"That's how ayahuasca poisoning works," don Fernando explained. "With alcohol, if you drink too much, you feel drunk or sick, but with ayahuasca, if you drink too much, you feel normal. You don't realize you've been poisoned."

Dan nodded his head.

"I have a doctor friend, Dani," don Fernando said. "He can detoxify you. It takes a couple of days, but he can cure you."

"Really?"

"Yes. You are lucky you realized it in time. If you had waited... well, it would be worse. Come, I will drive you there."

"Is he here in Villa Rosario?" Dan asked.

"Up in the hills a bit... not far."

"And this guy's a doctor?"

"Well... no... not a real doctor..." don Fernando said.

Dan frowned.

"But he's good, Dani. Trust me," don Fernando said.

Dan paused, but then said, "Okay, don Fernando... anything is better than last night."

Don Fernando opened his desk drawer and rifled through some papers until he found an old 3x5 card. Then he picked up his telephone and dialed the number that was on the card.

"Hola, don Emilio, this is Fernando... I'm am fine, thank you... I am bringing you a guest for a few days. Sí, Dani. In about twenty minutes. Thank you."

"You've talked to him about me before?" Dan blurted out after don Fernando hung up the phone.

"Of course, amigo. Come on, let's go."

"What about my clothes, toothbrush, etc.? Can we stop by my place?"

"You won't need any of that stuff," don Fernando said. "Everything you need will be there."

"Really?" Dan said. "Is this a clinic?"

"No, just his house. Come on."

Don Fernando stood up, took Dan's arm, and guided him out to his police car.

*   *   *

In the police car, Dan sat quietly. He wanted to tell don Fernando what had happened the night

before, but he didn't know how. He was afraid that don
Fernando would think he was insane. Actually, he was
worried that he *was* insane... and that if he described
what had happened to him the previous night, it would
somehow prove that he was insane.

Yesterday, while the police officer was driving
him back to Villa Rosario, he slept fitfully for most of
the ride, and woke up just as the officer was stopping
in front of his small apartment building. He mumbled
thanks to the officer, and climbed out of the car and
made his way up the stairs to his apartment. His
hands were shaking badly now. Even his arms were
twitching. He felt he had to have some ayahuasca to
calm himself. He went into his kitchen and opened the
refrigerator door and looked. There were four plastic
bottles of ayahuasca left. Enough for a couple of days...
maybe. But he didn't touch the bottles. He didn't want
to drink it. What had started off as an occasional
activity, a psychedelic diversion, a mystical experience
once or twice a month... had devolved into a daily
habit—first only at night, then night and morning, and
now every couple of hours. It had gotten out of hand.

Dan had once told don Fernando that ayahuasca
helped him to see things... and that was true. He could
connect dots with ayahuasca in a way that was never
possible before. But it had always a partnership—
him and ayahuasca. But now, somehow, the balance
of power had shifted. Ayahuasca was in control. He
closed the refrigerator door and went and lay down on
his bed.

It's not addictive, he told himself. It shouldn't
be. It doesn't contain any opioids... He tried to
reassure himself that it was just his own laziness,
his own weakness, his lack of discipline that had
created this dependency. He told himself he just
needed to be strong and not drink it for one day, and
he would feel fine again. He folded his hands over his
chest, interlocking his fingers, to try and control the
twitching. He closed his eyes and watched several
smoky colored rings spin in space. He took a deep

breath. He just needed to sleep.

Suddenly his apartment door burst open with an explosive bang! Dan's body jerked backward. It was as if the sound of the door bursting open had thrown his body against the headboard and was holding him there. He stared, unable to move. His apartment was filling up with men. At the front was Khambang, or rather, what was left of Khambang's badly decomposed body. Behind him were soldiers in camouflage uniforms and helmets, all fully armed. They rushed into the room, surrounded the bed, and grabbed Dan by his arms and legs. But their hands were small, with gnarly fingers. Dan looked at their faces—they weren't soldiers! They were pig men in soldier uniforms. Khambang seemed to be giving them directions by jerking his arms in spasmodic motions. The pig men held Dan against the headboard while other pig men searched through this apartment, opening drawers and dumping the contents on the floor and sorting through the piles. They dumped all the pots and pans out of the cupboards. They went into the bathroom, opened the medicine cabinet and dumped everything into the sink. They opened his closet, pulled down all the clothes and were going through all the pockets.

"What are they doing?!" Dan shouted at Khambang.

"They're looking for my children," was the answer that Dan heard Khambang say, even though nothing moved on the dead man's face. Dan saw that his lips were still sewn shut, and his eyes were closed.

"There's no children here!" Dan shouted back.

Khambang jerked his right shoulder up, and the pig men who were holding Dan started to pick him up off the bed and carried him out of the house and threw him over the balcony.

He was falling. But it was not the space in front of his apartment. Somehow he was in some other space, just falling. Far below him was a jungle.

Dan woke with a jerk. He looked around his

apartment. Nothing was in disarray. There had
been no pig men soldiers ransacking his drawers, no
Khambang giving orders like a broken scarecrow. Dan
sat up in bed, and rubbed his head, and said out loud,
"What the fuck?"

There was a knock on his door. He pulled
himself out of bed and went over to the door and
opened it. There stood Khambang. Behind him were
10 or 20 pig men soldiers. Dan slammed the door shut
and threw the deadbolt. He turned around. Khambang
and all the soldiers were in the room staring at him.
Dan screamed, turned back towards the door, opened
the deadbolt and the handle, and ran outside.

He was running through the jungle. It was the
middle of the night. It was hot, humid. Sweat was
dripping off him. He could feel insects buzzing all
around him. He ran until he was out of breath. Up
in the distance there was light from a clearing, from
a small fire. Dan walked towards it. He could see a
solitary figure standing over a small fire, stirring a
large cauldron with a wooden paddle. Dan knew from
the smell that it was a cauldron full of ayahuasca.
He also knew that the man stirring the pot was a
brujo. Dan looked around at the jungle. He had no
idea where he was. He walked up to the brujo. The
brujo dipped a tin cup into the ayahuasca mixture
and handed it to Dan. Dan blew on the steamy liquid
to cool it down and then took a sip. Leaves began to
sprout from his fingers. His hand began to turn woody
like the bark of a tree. His whole arm became hard
and numb. The numbness spread up to his shoulders.
He tried to turn but his feet were now welded to the
ground, taking root into the jungle soil.

Dan woke up tangled in the sheets. His right
arm had fallen asleep because of how he had been
lying on it. He sat up in the bed. His left hand was
twitching badly, but he used it to rub his right arm
to get the blood flowing. Slowly, sensation began to
return to his arm. As feeling came back, his right arm

began twitching. Well, he thought, at least he had feeling back in his arm. Plus the fact that his arm was numb from sleeping on it kind of explained the dream.

He looked over to the corner. Khambang was nailed to the wall like a crucifixion. "Oh fuck!" Dan said out loud. Was he caught in another dream? He looked around the apartment. But this was different. He wasn't asleep. He felt awake. Time was moving normally. He looked back to the corner. There was Khambang, still nailed to the wall, eyes closed, mouth sewn shut, head dangling over to one side. A terror began to overtake Dan. It was one thing to drink ayahuasca and see visions, but it was something completely different to have the visions invade his normal life. Khambang couldn't be in his apartment, but there he was. And this time Dan knew he wasn't dreaming.

He didn't want to look at the dead man. And he certainly didn't want to talk with him. It was enough to have the visual hallucination—he didn't want auditory hallucinations as well. He fought to keep the panic down. He thought to himself: "Okay, fine... I give up" and walked over to the refrigerator, grabbed one of the plastic bottles, opened it, took two big gulps of ayahuasca, and still holding the bottle, turned around and looked at the corner. Khambang was gone. He took the bottle over to the bed, placed it underneath the bed, and looked at the clock. Four a.m. Maybe he could get some sleep now. He looked at his hands. They were completely calm—no twitching. He lay down in the bed and fell asleep.

He awoke just before lunch. He had slept well since four. What a weird night, he thought to himself. He stretched in the bed, and brought his hands up in front of his eyes and looked at them. They were trembling with tiny shakes. He lifted his head and glanced over to the corner. There was Khambang, his arms outstretched, nailed to the wall. "Fuck no," he thought, and let his head drop back down. "I can't live like this." He rolled over on his right side reached down under the bed, found the bottle, brought it to his lips and took a sip, and let the smoky mixture slide down his throat. Then he turned and looked over to the corner. Khambang was gone. But Dan knew it was only temporary. He felt the panic starting to come back. Had he lost his mind? He got up, threw some clothes on, and went to see don Fernando.

* * *

"We're here, Dani," don Fernando said, as he pulled into the driveway of a small stucco house with a red tile roof.

Don Fernando shut off the car engine and got out. Dan opened his door and got out too. He felt like he was moving like a robot. He had set something into motion, but he wasn't sure what. But clearly, things were out of his control now. He had put himself in don Fernando's hands.

He followed don Fernando up to the front door. Don Fernando knocked. They both stood there, waiting. Don Fernando turned to Dan, smiled, and said, "It will be okay, Dani. Emilio knows what he's doing."

The door opened and a very old man gestured them to come in.

Once inside, don Fernando and the old man embraced. Then don Fernando introduced Dan.

"Dani, this is Doctor Emilio de la Cruz, one of my dearest friends. Emilio, this is Dani Landes, also one of my dearest friends."

Dan looked at the man whose hand he was shaking. He was an old man, at least eighty, Dan thought. Thin uncombed white hair, a scraggly face with white beard stubble, age spots on his cheeks and forehead, standing thin and stooped over... and yet his eyes seemed kind, almost sad.

"Come in and have a seat," Dr Cruz said, and gestured toward the small living room. "I've made some tea."

Dan and don Fernando took their seats on the couch while Dr. Cruz went into the kitchen and returned moments later with a tray. There were two small white china cups full of tea and one metal cup full of a darker liquid. Dr. Cruz handed a white cup to don Fernando and the metal cup to Dan. Then he took the remaining white cup and sat on the old chair opposite the couch.

"There's sugar in the bowl," he said to Dan, "but I don't think you'll need it. Your tea is naturally sweet."

Dan looked at the liquid in his cup. It was a dark brown, almost black. He glanced over at don Fernando's cup which held a light brown liquid. Dan blew on his cup to cool it, and took a sniff of the steam. It had a woody scent. Not unpleasant, but not like tea.

"What kind of tea is this?" Dan asked.

"It's a special detoxification herb tea. It actually tastes pretty good. Try it."

Dan took a little sip. It was sweet.

"Dani had a rough night last night," don Fernando said to Dr. Cruz.

"Ah, yes?" Dr. Cruz responded. "Got a bit too close to the veil?" he asked Dan.

Dan didn't understand. "The veil? What do you mean?"

"Ayahuasca allows us to see across the veil," the doctor explained. "But it does that by *thinning* the veil, so that it is transparent. The problem is, when you use ayahuasca too much, the veil gets too thin, and beings from the other side can see you."

Dr. Cruz was staring at Dan. "How do you like the tea?"

"It's okay," Dan said. "What's in it?"

"It's my own blend of plants and herbs... well, it's not my recipe. I learned it from the brujos in Peru

about sixty years ago. They've used it for centuries...
Drink it all."

Dan took another sip.

"Anyway, as I was saying, once the beings from
the other side can see you, they get curious and want
to cross the veil. That, of course, creates problems... I
assume you had some *visitors* last night, and it scared
you."

Dan nodded his head yes. He was starting to
feel trusting of this doctor. Here was someone who at
least understood. He was thankful don Fernando had
brought him here. At the same time he was starting to
feel just a bit dizzy. He looked at his hand. They were
calm.

"For now, we see through a glass, darkly; but
then face to face: now I know in part; but then shall I
know even as also I am known," the doctor said.

"What?" Dan said.

"One Corinthians, chapter 13, verse 12," Dr.
Cruz responded. "There is this human need to explore,
to always see what's on the other side, to always open
the forbidden door... it's natural. But people don't
always realize that the veil that separates us from the
other side actually serves two purposes. It keeps us
out, keeps us unaware, in the dark so to speak; but it
also keeps the other side out of our world. Finish your
tea."

Dan took the last sip of his cup. His stomach,
his whole body felt warm, tingly, but his head was
dizzy. "And what exactly is on the other side?" he
asked.

Dr. Cruz shrugged. "There's not really a word
for it... the future? the past? a combination of both?
Certainly some type of world that the gods didn't want
us to see."

Dan placed his empty tea cup on the table in
front of him.

"Ah, you've finished," Dr. Cruz said. "Good.
Perhaps you'd like to lie down for a few minutes.

Come, let me show you to your room."

Dr. Cruz stood up. Dan looked over at don Fernando. Don Fernando smiled, and nodded his head to indicate that Dan should follow Dr. Cruz.

Dan tried to stand up, but felt weak on his feet. Dr. Cruz grabbed him under one arm to steady him. Dan was amazed how strong Dr. Cruz's grip was. The man had seemed so frail when Dan first saw him; yet here Dan was, leaning on him.

Dr. Cruz walked Dan down a short hallway to a bedroom. He opened the door, switched on a light switch and guided Dan to the bed.

Dan was barely able to stand, but he looked around the room. It was small, and contained a bed and a small table by the bed. On the floor beside the table were three large trash cans lined with plastic bags.

Dr. Cruz helped Dan over to the bed and sat him down. Dan noticed the mattress was fitted with a plastic cover. On the table he saw five plastic bottles full of a red liquid.

"What's in the bottles?" he asked Dr. Cruz.

"Oh, that's a mixture of water, some electrolytes, sugar, some salt... It's like Gatorade in your country. You'll need to drink as much of it as you can today."

"Why?" Dan asked.

"Well, that tea you drank is very useful, very effective in counteracting the effects of ayahuasca, but it has one unpleasant side effect," Dr. Cruz said.

"Yes?"

"Well, you're going to be throwing up a lot over the next 24 hours... probably more than you have in your whole life. I would have told you before you drank it, but then... you wouldn't have drank it. Lie down here... when you need to vomit, use these big pails. Drink as much of the red bottled water as you can to keep from getting dehydrated. I'll replace the pails and the bottles as needed..."

Dan tried to stand up, saying, "I'm getting out of here!"

Dr. Cruz pushed Dan back down onto the bed with one finger. "Trust me," he said, "you haven't the energy to go anywhere."

It was true. Dan felt like all the energy to move had left his body. It was all he could do to just lie on the bed and breathe.

"So let me say again," Dr. Cruz continued, "how important it is to keep drinking the Gatorade mixture. I know you will think that it's insane to keep drinking and throwing the same liquid up, but believe me, it's important. Your body will absorb some of the water and electrolytes before you throw it up, and that will keep you alive. It's important to keep throwing up. It keeps the process working. I'll check in on you periodically and bring you new bottles of water as necessary."

Dan tried to say something, but he was too weak. A sense of nausea was starting to form in his stomach. Dr. Cruz patted Dan's arm, then stood up and walked out of the room.

Back out in the living room, don Fernando sat waiting patiently. Dr. Cruz came in and said: "More tea, Fernando?"

"Yes, don Emilio, that would be good. Thank you."

Dr. Cruz returned from the kitchen with the tea pot and refilled both don Fernando's cup and his own."

"So how's the wife and family?" Dr. Cruz asked.

"Doing very well, don Emilio, very well. Gracias a Dios, I am truly blessed."

The two men continued talking. The walls muffled the sound of Dan's vomiting.

Chapter 12

There was an ex-cop from the states
who was good at tempting the fates,
but the road of excess
creates quite a mess
as it leads all the way to the gates.

It had been five days since Ricardo had taken Marco to his apartment. He had promised Marco that he would talk to Dan, or at least try and find out something about this guy who died in Marco's hotel—something that would reassure Marco—but so far he hadn't been able to find Dan. He had called his number, but there was no answer. He had checked Dan's favorite restaurants, but no one had seen him recently. He had even gone by his apartment one time, but there was no one home. But Villa Rosario was a small town, so Ricardo wasn't worried. Sooner or later, he would run into him.

*   *   *

Dr. Vargas peered through the microscope at the tissue sample. It seemed to be growing quite fast, very fast. She had built a small incubator in her kitchen at home, so that no one at the lab would know what she was doing. But now she would have to build a larger incubator.

*   *   *

Puii was excited. Krasko was going to bring the Bulgarian girls over to the farmhouse for sex later that evening. It was about time, Puii thought. He had sent Rune into Villa Rosario to get buy alcohol and snacks for the party, and to stop by the butcher shop to get more pig blood for the incubators.

* * *

Rune parked Krasko's van on a side road by the mercado on the far edge of town. There was a closer store for alcohol, but this mercado had a pay phone inside that actually had some privacy. Rune looked around. It was midday and hot, so few people were out shopping. He went inside, nodded at the cashier, and went into the back to the pay phone. He picked up the receiver and dialed a long series of numbers which he knew by heart—numbers that connected to the local phone exchange which connected to the Panamanian phone service, which connected to an international operator—numbers that allowed him to call for free, so that his voice could travel thousands of miles.

Somewhere in the Armed Forces Security Center in Thailand, a phone started ringing.

* * *

"Here, have some soup."
Dan opened his eyes. Dr. Cruz was sitting on the edge of his bed, holding a small steaming bowl of something and a spoon.
"Come on, it's good soup. I think you're ready to eat a little," Dr. Cruz said.
Dan looked around. He simply had no idea what day it was. He knew where he was. He recognized Dr. Cruz. He knew that his body had never felt so pummeled. It was as if he had been run over by a tank. But he had no idea of how long he had been there.
"Come on, try a sip." Dr. Cruz held out a spoonful of soup.
Dan opened his mouth like a child and took the spoon. His throat felt raw, but the soup tasted good.
"It's just chicken broth, but it'll give you strength.

Tomorrow, we'll try some solid food. But for right now, this is sufficient."

Dan nodded. He positioned his arms and pushed himself up to a sitting position, and took the bowl and spoon that Dr. Cruz held out to him. He took small sips of the soup, savoring the flavor. He hoped it would stay down.

"Bits of memory will come back to you slowly, over the next few days. It takes a few days to get all your strength back. But the good news is, the ayahuasca is out of your system. You won't have any more *visitors* from the other side."

Dan nodded and continued taking sips of soup.

"Ayahuasca is a most amazing drug," Dr. Cruz continued. "On one hand, it's simply a plant containing certain alkaloids that block the reabsorption of serotonin by the serotonin transporter neurons in the brain. That's the scientific view, anyway. On the other hand, as brujos have known for centuries, it is a gift from the gods that allows us to see into the other side. Everyone who becomes a devotee of ayahuasca learns to see past the veil, into both the past and future. But ayahuasca comes with strings attached, my friend, as you found out. Which is why the ancient brujos believed that the herbal tea that you drank the other day was also a gift of the gods, a way of repairing the veil. But it also comes with strings attached... as you also found out. It is, shall we say, hard to stomach."

Dan winced at Dr. Cruz's little joke about the vomiting. He looked around the room. Someone had obviously cleaned up. The plastic lined trash cans were gone. The bottles of red water were gone. Dan could only remember hours and hours of vomiting, vomiting and crying, and then feeling thirsty, and drinking the red water, only to vomit it out again. It seemed to go on forever.

He wanted to ask Dr. Cruz how long he had been here. He opened his mouth, but found it painful to try and make a sound.

"No, no, don't try and talk," Dr. Cruz said. "Just try

and rest. Sleep if you can. I'll bring you some more soup later."

* * *

Jorge Manuel was feeling frustrated. His case felt like it was at standstill. It had been three days since they had discovered the two murdered Brazilian girls, three days since they had searched the abandoned villa outside of La Chorrera. How were these murderers always one step ahead of him? Was he missing some clues? Was he a bad police chief? He had lost the original body and the ice chest. He blamed himself for not arresting the two Brazilian girls after they had returned to the apartment. He blamed himself for not being able to get better maps out of the two Colombian girls. Maybe he should have put them in the police cars to direct them when they were looking for the bright yellow house. The FBI was lying to him. The Thai consulado wouldn't talk to him unless he was mad about something. When he tried to talk to don Fernando about how he was feeling, his uncle just laughed and told him he was doing a fine job.

He had shown the two Colombian girls the photos of their murdered roommates. They both cried, of course. But they agreed to stay in the jail after Jorge Manuel had explained it was for their own safety. He did give them each a TV so they wouldn't be bored.

* * *

The next day, Dr. Cruz called don Fernando and told him that Dan was cured and ready to go home.

"Ah bueno, don Emilio, that is good to hear," don Fernando had said. "I'll be there in twenty minutes."

When don Fernando pulled up in front of Dr. Cruz's house, Dan and Dr. Cruz were standing outside waiting for him.

"Hola Dani," don Fernando called out. "Cómo estás?"

"I'm good, don Fernando. In fact, you're looking at a

141

proud graduate of the best Weight Watchers Program in the world," Dan replied.

"Qué?" don Fernando said.

"Sorry," Dan replied, "a little joke. I'm fine, don Fernando."

Dan turned to Dr. Cruz and said simply, "Thank you, doctor."

"Mucho gusto, Señor Landes. Try and remember all the things we discussed this morning."

"Oh, I will, doctor. I will."

Dan climbed into the passenger side of don Fernando's patrol car. Both he and don Fernando waved at Dr. Cruz as they drove away.

"I assume you want to go home," don Fernando said.

"Actually, don Fernando, can you take me to a restaurant, any restaurant? Dr. Cruz is a good doctor, but he's a terrible cook. I am so hungry."

* * *

Later that afternoon, after don Fernando took Dan to have lunch together at Mariscos, and after he dropped him off at his apartment, don Fernando got a telephone call from his nephew.

Don Fernando hadn't told Jorge Manuel that Dan was under Dr. Cruz's care, of course. He had only told his nephew that Dan was out of town. So when Jorge Manuel inquired if Dan had returned, don Fernando only said, "Sí, he has returned, but he is tired from traveling. He may need a day or two to rest, Koke."

"I understand, uncle. I was just hoping the three of us could get together soon and discuss this case."

"Ah, are there any new developments?" don Fernando asked.

"No," Jorge Manuel admitted. "There are none. I feel completely stymied. It's as if the three blonde prostitutes have disappeared into thin air. My officers have talked to all the prostitutes in La Chorrera, but no one has seen them. Even Jenny doesn't know where they are. Without finding them, I don't know how we can find the three men."

"Patience, Koke," don Fernando said. "Something will turn up. It may be that they have all left Panama. But my experience is that criminals always come back to their old neighborhoods. We just need to wait and be patient. As long as no more bodies turn up, things are good. In the meantime, send your officers to all the hotels in town. Have them meet quietly with the hotel managers and tell them to report if any turistas bring a blonde 'guest' over for a night."

"Sí, uncle, I will do that."

"And how did the interview with the owner of that big yellow house go?" don Fernando asked.

"Just as we thought, uncle. He didn't know anything. The Bulgarian man always paid him in cash so the owner didn't do a reference check or anything. The Bulgarian told them they were missionaries and wanted their privacy so the owner never went to the place. He didn't even know they had moved out."

"Okay, Koke. Well, let's just be patient. Call me if anything new happens, and then I will arrange a lunch with Dani and the three of us will talk."

"Okay uncle, thank you."

Chapter 13

There was a young lady from Panama
who strayed from medical protocol,
but the things in her kitchen
were like science fiction,
and she feared she had broken God's law.

Jorge Manuel tried to be patient, but over the next two weeks, there were just no new developments in the case. At least, not in La Chorrera...

But in the small farmhouse outside of Villa Rosario, things were happening. Krasko had just arrived from a trip to the airport in Panama City. Puii went outside when he heard Krasko's van pull up.

Krasko hopped out of the van, went around to the side, and opened the sliding door. The inside was crammed full of large shipping bins with big red crosses on the sides.

"Help me carry these inside," he said to Puii.

"What are those?" Puii asked.

"New shipping containers from Ravanco," Krasko answered. "They built them special for us."

Krasko pulled one out, placed it on the ground, undid the top latch, and flipped open the lid. "See how the incubators will each fit in these slots? Each one has its own temperature control. And these are tiny battery-powered fans with water misters that will keep them moist; and these are the feeding tubes that fit into these bags for blood."

Puii peered into the bin. "Very ingenious," he said.

"By the way," Krasko asked, "where is Rune? We could use some help."

"He said something about taking a walk," Puii said. "He said he was bored."

"That dumbfuck," Krasko said. "He needs to stay inside the farmhouse. I don't care how bored he is. We need to lay low out here. Well, come on, let's get these bins into the house."

Krasko and Puii carried the bins into the house, one at a time. Puii had not realized, until they had unloaded them, how many bins there were. He counted them and did some quick mental calculations.

Then he asked Krasko, "You're still planning to do three shipments, right?"

"Nope," Krasko said. "That's the beauty of this new design. We can ship all the product in one shipment. I'm aiming for next week."

A huge knot formed in the pit of Puii's stomach. He had been counting on what Krasko had told him two weeks ago about moving the product in three shipments. He and Afzaal had worked out a plan—that while Krasko would be flying to the Dominican Republic with the first shipment, Puii was going to move the rest of the incubators to a location in Panama City. Afzaal was then going to fly to Panama, deposit ten million dollars in Puii's Mossack Fonseca account, and take the incubators back to Pakistan. Now, that whole plan was totally fucked! He would have to let Afzaal know. He would have to come up with a new plan!

* * *

It had taken Dan two weeks to get adjusted to his new ayahuasca-free lifestyle. But he was sleeping better, eating better, and most importantly, he was not seeing things that weren't there. He felt ready to delve back into the case, but don Fernando had informed him that there had simply been no new developments—no more dead bodies, no sign of the Bulgarian and the two Asians, and no sign of the three blonde prostitutes.

But then Dan got a call from Dr. Vargas late in the afternoon.

"We need to talk," she said tersely. "Can you come by tomorrow morning?"

"I'll be there," Dan replied.

"Thanks," she said, and hung up.

A woman of few words, Dan thought to himself and smiled.

But he didn't want to have one of don Fernando's officers drive him again, so the next morning, he just got up early and caught the bus from Villa Rosario to Panama City.

Bus rides for Dan were always a time to reflect. Something about being a passenger with nothing to do but watch the scenery go by, experiencing the rhythmic bumps of the road, stopping and waiting for passengers to get on or off, not really knowing the person who was driving the bus... something about the entire experience being outside of his control, always led Dan to reflect on his life: how he had ended up in Villa Rosario from his desk job as a white collar crime detective in the Crenshaw District of the L.A. police force. Like the bus ride he was on, his journey to Panama had been a long bumpy road. Still, despite all the hardships, he had no regrets. He really loved Panama.

Most people don't end up in life where they had planned to end up. Some are like Dan, and end up in the *location* they had envisioned, but not being the *type of person* they thought they would be. Dan had first visited Panama right after college, and had come back every vacation he could. Somewhere in his heart, he always knew that he would retire here. And the fates had allowed him to do that. But he had always assumed his personality would stay the same, that his view of the world would stay the same. He had been a good cop back in L.A.—at least he had thought so—he had been studious and meticulous, and had tried to just keep his head down and do his job according to his own sense of ethics. So he had assumed that he would retire to Panama, and live a quiet life, maybe even marry a nice Panameña woman... and he would putter around garden during the day and she would cook old-fashioned Panamanian food. But none of that had happened. It would be easy to blame ayahuasca for his difficulties of late. But in reality he knew that his difficulties were of his own making, and ayahuasca was just his way of coping with the choices he continued to make. He couldn't honestly say anymore that he was a good, ethical cop. He was just an ex-cop, not so good, not so ethical, but still trying.

His thoughts turned to the reason he was on the bus... the tissue that he had left with Dr. Vargas. He wondered what had prompted her to call him. What was it about that tissue that made people want to kill other people for it?

He looked out the window and watched the scenery go by. Even though the molecules of ayahuasca were out of his system, they had left their tattoos, their memories. In his mind's eye, he saw the slums of Mumbai. He had this image of Krasko and Puii enticing homeless young men into an anonymous factory building with the promise of a job, and then sedating them and injecting them with early versions of the pig tissue. They dragged the comatose men to cells, fed them food and water for several days, and watched what happened.

A shiver ran through Dan's body. People are no damn good, he thought to himself.

* * *

Dr. Vargas was in the lobby when Dan entered the building.

"Thank you for coming to meet me," she said and shook his hand.

Dan realized that this was the first time they had touched. He liked the feel of her hand. It was warm, with soft skin. But he noticed the worried look on her face.

They went upstairs, this time to a small office with a desk. She took a seat behind the desk, and he sat down in a chair facing her.

She started right in: "I've never seen anything like this tissue, Señor Landes... In fact, I don't think there is anything like this in the history of biology. This tissue... this biological hazard... is so dangerous..."

She seemed at a loss for words, but Dan didn't know what question to ask, so he sat quietly and just waited. After a moment, she started again.

"There have always been viruses that kill tissue. And there have always been parasites that feed on tissue. And certainly, the history of evolution—of life itself—depends on each species feeding off of other plant or animal species... But this tissue combines all of those features. I wish I had destroyed the samples you gave me... but I was curious... so I set up a small incubator in my house and simply observed it. If I did nothing, just kept it warm and moist—it survived, not growing, but not dying either, as if it was in a state of hibernation. Out of curiosity—it was something you said about the Greek myth of Saturn—I mixed a little pig blood into one of the Petri dishes with the tissue and watched under the microscope. Any kind of blood seems to trigger something. This tissue attacks any blood cells or tissue cells, but it doesn't just kill it—it consumes it and converts it into more tissue. It grows by consuming other species' blood or tissue. And it didn't matter what type of blood or tissue I put in the dishes—chicken blood, cow blood... I even poked my own finger and put a few drops in a Petri dish. It fed on that, too... It's like vampire tissue..."

She paused again. "But that's not what scares me. I found that I could control the rate of growth by simply controlling the amount of blood I fed it. If I gave it just a minimal amount of blood, it grew, simply by feeding and dividing—it grew fast—superfast, like a cancer—but it was *only* growing—just replicating—not evolving. *But*... when I doused it with blood, submerged it, gave it as much blood as it wanted, it began, not simply to divide, but to form blastulas!"

Dan frowned. He wasn't sure what she meant.

"Blastulas," she repeated. "The beginning of human embryos! Remember, these were stem cells to start with. Suddenly, when it had enough food, it began to develop into an embryo—at alarming speed. I started off with one incubator—now I have four! Within twelve hours of drenching the embryos in blood, I could detect a vertebrate body plan... another six hours, the beginning of organ systems... another six hours... and it began to look like a human embryo, but with a larger head and mouth, eating constantly. Within another twelve hours you could see them with the naked eye, just swimming in all that blood, sucking it up and growing superfast."

Dr. Vargas' face looked horrified as she uttered those words. It was the first time she had said them out loud, and the reality of them frightened her.

Dan leaned all the way back in the chair and let his head fall back against the headrest. He stared at the space up towards the ceiling, seeing, once again, the slums of Mumbai stretching out before him. Thousands of tiny shanty houses, thousands of poor destitute people, thousands of mouths to feed... At that moment, the thousand patterns of what it all meant clicked together in his head. Even without ayahuasca, or maybe because of ayahuasca's chemical tattoos on his brain, Dan was connecting the dots.

"But that's not the worst part," Dr. Vargas said. "I started experimenting with seeing what types of food, besides blood, they would consume. I was gradually introducing bigger pieces of food: bits of hamburger, meat, fat, anything... and they would eat anything. And they continue to grow. By yesterday morning, these embryos were almost one inch in length, with little arms and legs... and for some ungodly reason—I don't know why—I began to wonder what they would do with something more complex than hamburger, so I put a live tadpole into the bloodbath... and they attacked it, and they attacked it as a group. It was as if they were working together, trying to eat it. It was horrible."

She looked like she was going to cry. She looked at him and said, "What in God's name are these things?"

"They're soldiers," Dan said. "I suppose you could call them vampire or zombie pig soldiers. But they're soldiers. Those fucking maniacs figured out how to grow the perfect soldier. You don't have to train them or even feed them—you just have to turn them loose."

"I don't understand," Dr. Vargas said.

"What makes the world go round, Doctor? It's not love—it's war. It's cheap to make armaments, but it's expensive to train soldiers. That's why the world had gone more and more to drones and bombs over the past 30 years. But drones and bombs can't fight ground wars. You've seen how terrorism has grown worldwide. You've got to have boots on the ground. So what these assholes did was to genetically modify stem cells to produce test-tube soldiers. With this tissue they can grow full adult soldiers in one year in a laboratory. They've rewired their brains so they work in groups to kill and eat the enemy. It's the start of a new kind of war—an Armageddon War. Whoever controls this tissue can rule the world... by destroying everyone else."

Dr. Vargas sat silently, her mouth opened. Dan sat and thought, then said, "You have to destroy all that tissue, doctor."

She looked at him. "I can't do that. Those are human embryos!"

"No they're not, doctor. Those are monster embryos. Where is all the tissue now?"

"At my house."

He looked at her. He understood her confusion, her being conflicted.

"Take me there," he said. "I'll dispose of the tissue."

She sat there, thinking.

"Doctor," Dan said, "what those creatures did to that tadpole, they will do to any living creature. Full grown, they will eat men, women, and children. We cannot let them grow anymore. They have to be destroyed."

"You'll do it?" she asked quietly.

Dan nodded his head yes.

"Okay," she said quietly, and stood up. "I'll take you there."

*　*　*

Dr. Vargas lived in a small but nice house on the outskirts of Panama City. Like all the houses in the neighborhood, it was surrounded by iron gates. She pulled her car into her garage and got out and locked the gate. Dan got out of the car and followed her inside the house.

"Nice place," he said after they stepped inside and

walked through the living room.

"Thank you," she said, "I inherited it after my mother died last year. Follow me, the kitchen is over here."

Like most Panamanian homes, the kitchen was huge. But the counters were full of square metal roasting pans. Dan peered into one. There was a pool of blood about three inches deep with small creatures bobbing in it.

He counted four roasting pans. "Is this all the tissue?" he asked.

"No," she said, "these four bins are just from one piece of glass. The rest of the glass pieces with tissue are over there." She pointed to a smaller covered round metal stew pot.

"Okay," Dan said and then paused. He realized that he hadn't thought about *how* he was going to kill the pig embryos.

"Do you have a back yard?" he asked.

She looked at him confused, but said, "Yes."

"Show me."

Dan followed her through the living room, down a hall, to a back door. There was a small unfinished cement patio, which opened onto a huge back yard, surrounded by a high fence. A pile of bricks was stacked next to the house.

"Building a patio?" he asked and smiled.

"My mother was having it done. I haven't had time to have it completed."

Dan looked beyond the fence. No neighbor could see in. The yard seemed to back up against a vacant field.

"This is perfect," he said. "Do you have a small shovel or garden trowel?"

She brought him a shovel. He dug a wide circular pit about ten inches deep in the middle of the yard away from the patio, then lined the edges with some of the bricks from the side of the patio.

"Do you have some paper? Old newspaper or something?" he asked.

She brought him some paper bags. He tore them up and threw them into the pit. Then he gathered some sticks and small pieces of wood from the sides of the yard.

She brought him a small lighter without being asked.

He started the paper burning and blew on it to get the wood going.

"Your very own fire pit," he said. "But I'm going to need more wood."

"There's some scrap lumber in the garage," she said, "I'll bring it to you."

"Yes, bring all you got."

While she was carrying wood scraps from the garage, Dan went into the kitchen and brought the first of the four roasting pans out to the fire. One by one he carried the bins out, and then finally he carried out the stew pot that held the broken pieces of glass.

He dumped some of the wood that she brought from the garage onto the fire. There was a nice blaze going now.

He needed something to fish the embryos out. He went into the kitchen and found a wooden slotted spoon in one of the drawers.

Dr. Vargas eyes widened when she saw the wooden spoon. She knew he was going to fish the embryos out with it.

"I can't watch," she said, and turned to go inside. "Please burn that spoon when you are done."

Dan started skimming through the blood of the first bin and dumping the tiny embryos into the fire. They crackled, hissed, and twisted up when they hit the flames. He didn't care. He was beyond caring now. He kept skimming the wooden spoon through the blood. When he felt sure that one roasting pan was empty, he went to the next one. One by one he skimmed out every embryo and tossed it into the fire. When the fire got low, he added more wood. After almost forty minutes, when he felt that he had caught every embryo, he removed the lid of the stew pot and dumped the pieces of broken glass onto the fire. The glass pieces blackened. Most of them cracked into smaller pieces. He threw more wood onto the fire, including the wooden spoon. Then he carefully poured the blood from three of the roasting pans into the fourth pan, and then set the fourth pan directly onto the fire. He stoked the fire under the pan with more wood. Slowly the blood began to steam, and then finally boil. Dan pulled a chair from off the patio and sat upwind of the smoke and watched the blood burn away.

When the blood was completely burned off, he took each of the four bins and the round pot and leaned them into the fire so that flames would scorch the inside. Then he sat back in his chair and waited for the fire to burn down.

It was nighttime now. Stars were beginning to come out. Dr. Vargas came outside.

"Is it done?" she asked.

"Yes," he said.

She looked up at the dark sky. He heard her sigh. "It's pretty out here tonight, Señor Landes," she said softly.

Dan looked up at the stars. Their points of light were bright and vast.

"Yes, it is," he said, and then added, "and María... please call me Dan."

She nodded and walked over to the patio and brought one of the chairs over and placed it next to Dan's. Then she turned and went back into the house.

A minute later she returned with two glasses of wine, and held one out to Dan. He took it.

"Thanks," he said, "I could use this."

She sat down next to him.

"Señor Landes... I mean Dan," she started. "I feel so bad. I should never have incubated that tissue. I was just so curious. But now I feel so horrible, like I have sinned. And you had to kill those babies and it is all my fault. I don't think God will ever forgive me."

"Well... María..." Dan said, "in the first place, those weren't babies. They were man-made, genetically-engineered piranha pig-mutant fucked-up pieces of hell. They were devil tissue. If God exists, He will create a special place in heaven for you. If you had not incubated that tissue, we would never have known that those maniacs were creating... No, you should not feel bad. You should feel proud."

"How can I feel proud for breaking every ethical code of my profession?" she asked. "First I grew human life, and then I let you kill it."

Dan reached over and placed his hand on her left

arm. "Believe me, María, it wasn't human. These creatures were not created by love—they were created by hate and by greed. And they weren't created—they were manufactured, prefabricated by mixing DNA and chemicals. Please, understand... the ethical code they taught you in school or in church is outmoded—it never envisioned these conditions. There is no ethical code that fits these conditions... this type of evil... believe me, we did the right thing... the only thing."

She slid her arm up to take his hand in hers, and held it while she took a sip of her wine with her other hand.

As the fire began to die down, they could see more and more stars. They both leaned back, holding hands, and watched the sky. They were both feeling lost and desolate in their own private thoughts, and yet, somehow, as they caressed each other's hands, a bit of hope began to emerge, a tiny bit of goodness...

Chapter 14

The third young man from Thailand
was embedded into the scam.
Sent in undercover,
he was never discovered,
until he revealed his own plan.

The next morning, while Dan was riding the bus back to Villa Rosario, Puii was walking through the farmhouse looking for Rune. He called his name and peered into each room. There was no answer. Puii thought that was strange.

Puii heard Krasko's voice behind him. "I sent him into town."

"Oh?" Puii said.

"Yes, I told him to pick up a few things," Krasko said.

Puii didn't think they needed any new supplies, but he decided that this was as good of an opportunity as any to talk with Krasko.

"Okay, well good, um... listen, Krasko, I think I need to take a quick trip to Mumbai. I got a text from them this morning and they're having problems with the growth rate on the new starter tissue. They don't know what's wrong and asked me to come. I checked the airline schedule. If I fly out tonight, I can be back here in four days."

"No need," Krasko said. "I know what's wrong with the starter tissue in Mumbai."

Puii felt a knot of panic in his stomach. "You do?" he asked.

"Yes, I do. The problem is, there isn't any starter tissue left in Mumbai. I had it eradicated two days ago."

"What?!!" exclaimed Puii. "You destroyed the starter tissue? Why?!!"

"To make this shipment more valuable, of course," Krasko said, pulling his Ruger pistol out of his shoulder holster and aiming at Puii. "And I know all about your texts from Mumbai... Only they're not from Mumbai, are they? They're from Karachi, from some friends of yours. You were going to try to undercut me, weren't you, Puii? Fly to Mumbai, my ass. You were going to steal some of this product, and work your own deal."

Puii stared at the pistol in Krasko's hand. He held his hands up in front of him and started to say "No" when Krasko pulled the trigger.

Krasko liked the Ruger .22 because it was small and light, easy to conceal, and very reliable. But he also knew it didn't pack a lot of firepower. After all, it was only a .22 caliber. But its magazine held ten rounds. He put four into Puii's chest, and then walked over to where Puii was writhing on the floor, and put two more into Puii's head.

"That should do it," Krasko thought to himself. "Gads, what a bloody mess. Now I just have to wait for Rune to show back up."

Krasko went into the living room and opened the front door so he could get a good view of the driveway. Then he slid one of the big chairs across the floor to position it, and sat down. While he waited, he refilled the Ruger's magazine and then placed the pistol back in his holster. He took out a cigar, lit it, and waited.

* * *

Dan had called don Fernando from his cell phone when he had left Panama City, and asked him to arrange a lunch in Villa Rosario with Jorge Manuel.

"Do you want to eat at Mariscos?" don Fernando asked.

"No, let's go to a real restaurant," Dan said, "Let's meet at noon at El Balcón."

But as Dan rode the bus back to Villa Rosario, he

pondered exactly what he was going to tell don Fernando and Jorge Manuel. He had felt the need to bring everyone into the loop; to explain what the tissue was; to put their heads together and try and figure out the next step; to explain how important it was to find this Bulgarian and the two Thai thugs; but he certainly wasn't going to tell them that he had spent the night with María José Vargas, and he certainly wasn't going to explain that she had grown the tissue, or that he had destroyed it... So he wasn't sure *how* he was going to explain how he knew what he knew.

But it turned out that Dan didn't need to worry about how to explain what María had grown in her kitchen laboratory. Because it was in that tiny upstairs restaurant that Ricardo's orbit was about to collide with Dan's.

When Dan showed up at El Balcón, don Fernando and Jorge Manuel were already there, sitting at a small table on the balcony. Dan greeted both of them affectionately. Maybe it was the flood of new serotonins in his system from the night of lovemaking—serotonins not being hijacked by the ayahuasca molecules—that made him feel especially friendly towards his two friends. But he was glad to see them and his mood was good.

Don Fernando noted Dan's warmth and felt pleased that he had taken him to see Dr. Cruz. This was the old Dan that he had known for so many years.

The three man ordered coffee and tea, and perused the menu. When the waiter returned, they all ordered lunch. Then Jorge Manuel started discussing what little progress they had made.

It was at that moment that Ricardo walked into the restaurant.

Now, Dan was aware that El Balcón was Ricardo's favorite restaurant in Villa Rosario. In fact, it was Ricardo who, years ago, had first taken Dan to El Balcón, and he and Ricardo had eaten there many times. And so Dan knew, earlier that morning when he suggested it to don Fernando as a place to meet, that there would be some chance that he would see Ricardo there. But the fact was, there were very few decent restaurants in Villa Rosario, so Dan was willing to take that chance. He simply thought that if they did run into Ricardo, that he would explain to Ricardo that they were there to discuss business, so he couldn't invite Ricardo to join them.

And so when Ricardo saw Dan and waved and walked over to say hello, Dan stood up politely and smiled, glad to see his friend, but with the intent to explain why he couldn't ask Ricardo to sit with them. And Ricardo walked up, and he and Dan were just talking, exchanging pleasantries, and don Fernando and Jorge Manuel were continuing to talk to each other... and it was one of those moments, dear Reader, one of those serendipitous moments, when Dan was starting to explain that they were there to discuss business, just as Jorge Manuel was saying to don Fernando, "I only wish we knew where those three blondes went."

The human brain is an amazing thing—it's always processing—and the rest of the human organs are constantly feeding that brain with information, most of it beneath our consciousness. Because it was also true that at the moment that Dan was walking up to their table, Jorge Manuel had used the words "Thai" and "Bulgarian" and maybe even the phrase "dead man"... and although Ricardo did not consciously hear those words, the fact is, the sound waves carrying those words originated only several feet from Ricardo, and those invisible sound waves certainly reached Ricardo and washed over him and continued for several feet past him. And while those few words alone would not have been enough for anyone's rational mind to understand the context or history of what Jorge Manuel was saying to don Fernando, Ricardo's unconscious mind, always working, always processing—just like yours and my mind—had already taken those few words and had compared them with other memories of hearing those same words in the recent past, and had made a match with the conversation that Ricardo had had with Marco just two weeks earlier, and another match to the memory of Miguel telling him about the meeting of these same three men in his restaurant to discuss the murder of the man in

Marco's hotel...

Now, nothing in Ricardo's rational mind was making these connections. It was just that Jorge Manuel had uttered that sentence "I only wish we knew where those three blondes went" at the exact moment when there was a short pause in Ricardo's speaking with Dan, so that those words were audible to Ricardo's conscious brain, just at the point when he was about to turn and greet don Fernando and Jorge Manuel. And Ricardo's brain, which had already processed the words "Thai" and "Bulgarian" and "dead man" unconsciously, now upon hearing "I only wish we knew where those three blondes went" at the exact moment that he was about to say something to the other two men... all these events came together so that Ricardo said, "You're not talking about those three prostitutes from La Chorrera, are you?"

And of course, all three men looked at Ricardo dumbfounded, as if he was clairvoyant. But Ricardo's unconscious brain, still processing, saw the micro-movement of a yes nod from Jorge Manuel's head, so he added: "Oh, I know where they are."

Dan was the first to regain his composure. "Where are they, Ricardo?"

"Some Asian man checked them into the Monteverde Vista Hotel here in town two weeks ago."

Dan looked at don Fernando and Jorge Manuel. Ricardo was about to say that he assumed that they were still there, because at that moment, his rational brain was starting to censor... starting to realize what a bizarre thing it was that he had just said, so he wanted to start qualifying it, but he never got the chance.

"Let's go," Dan exclaimed, and Jorge Manuel and don Fernando jumped up. Dan grabbed Ricardo's arm, and said quickly, "Come with us. If you're right, we'll buy your lunch later."

The three men ran out of the restaurant, dragging Ricardo with them. Don Fernando yelled at the waiter as they ran out to hold their orders.

They all piled into don Fernando's patrol car parked

out front and sped over to the Monteverde Vista. Don Fernando called the station for back-up and a transport van to meet them at the hotel. Don Fernando was driving fast, his police lights going, but with the siren off.

"Dani," don Fernando shouted, "What are we arresting them for?"

"Doesn't matter," Dan shouted back. "Let's just hope we find them alive."

Then Dan turned to Ricardo and exclaimed, "How do you know about them?"

Ricardo was at a loss for words. He had promised Marco he wouldn't get him involved, and he certainly didn't want to get Miguel in trouble for eavesdropping on the detectives' conversation in his restaurant several weeks ago.

So he just blurted out, "Everybody knows."

Dan and Jorge Manuel just stared at Ricardo in disbelief.

"What?" Dan exclaimed.

"You're talking about the three blonde hookers who work for the Asian guys in La Chorrera, right?" Ricardo asked.

"Yeah?" Dan said.

"Well, everyone knows they moved them here after that guy died in that hotel."

Jorge Manuel just shook his head. Clearly he was a failure at being a police chief, if everyone knew what he couldn't find out after weeks of investigation.

Dan stared at Ricardo, but intuited that Ricardo wasn't being honest.

"Bullshit," Dan said. "Everybody doesn't know."

"Well, yeah, okay," Ricardo admitted. "Not *everyone*."

"How did you know?" Dan asked slowly.

"A friend of mine saw an Asian guy check them into the hotel. My friend told me. That's all, Dan. Honestly."

Dan nodded. That made more sense to him. Dan looked down at the car's floorboards and tried to think. He could feel that events were suddenly about to explode, like a huge tidal wave held in place solely by the fact that it was in the future and not in the present second of time.

He wished he had some ayahuasca. He remembered what a brujo had once told him about using ayahuasca... "Once a devotee, always a devotee." He closed his eyes and tried to will the clarity of mind that came when let that sweet smoky liquid slide down his throat. He could see the slums of Mumbai stretching out before him in some vast stark war zone. He could see hordes of pig soldiers feasting on the bodies of everyone they had shot. He could feel treachery and betrayal unfolding.

He felt the car stop. They had pulled up in front of the hotel.

"You stay here," Dan said to Ricardo. Dan and Jorge Manuel and don Fernando jumped out of the car and raced up the stairs into the hotel lobby.

Don Fernando flashed his badge at the desk clerk and yelled, "The three blonde girls that checked in two weeks ago, are they still here?"

The desk clerk seemed frozen, unable to speak. Don Fernando unsnapped the safety strap across his belt holster, and the desk clerk found his voice. "Yes, sir, room 405."

"Anyone with them right now?" Dan yelled.

The desk clerk shook his head no.

Don Fernando and Jorge Manuel dashed toward the elevator. Dan stayed standing in front of the desk clerk, partly to make sure he didn't call the girls, and partly to ask him questions.

Dan smiled at the desk clerk, but then said in as cold of a voice as he could muster, "Señor, you are not in any trouble, as long as you speak honestly with us. Do you understand?"

The desk clerk nodded his head.

"An Asian man checked these girls in, about two weeks ago?"

The desk clerk nodded again.

"And a big gringo comes to visit them occasionally?"

Again the nod yes.

"Do they get many visitors?"

The desk clerk looked nervous.

"Male visitors?"

Now the desk clerk was very nervous.

"I promise you, señor, you are not in any trouble," Dan said again. "One more question... the big gringo, he occasionally slips you some money, yes?"

Dan could see beads of sweat forming on the desk clerk's forehead. Dan said, "I'll take that as a yes."

Several policemen ran into the lobby from two patrol cars that had just pulled up out front. Dan waved them over and said, "Room 405." They ran down the hall.

Dan thought for a moment. His mind was running a rapid calculation of all the possible outcomes that could occur. In a world of infinite possibilities, Krasko and the two Thai men could be anywhere. But people are creatures of habit. Krasko had housed the three Bulgarian hookers in La Chorrera so he could pimp them out, and he had kept a villa on the outskirts of that town so he could have privacy but still be near the girls. So he probably was doing the same thing here. Somewhere outside of Villa Rosario, he had probably rented a house. Krasko also liked to bring the Colombian prostitutes to his villa for sex, so it was likely he was using these girls the same way, which meant they knew where he was.

He looked up at the desk clerk. "Can I borrow a piece of paper and a pen?"

The desk clerk pulled a sheet of paper and a pen from a drawer and held it out to Dan.

"No, just leave it on the counter. Thank you," Dan said.

Down the hallway from the elevator came Jorge Manuel, don Fernando, and the other cops holding the three blonde girls by the arms. The women were handcuffed, with their arms behind their backs. The tallest blonde was shouting, "We want a lawyer. We know our rights! We want a lawyer."

Dan gestured for don Fernando to stop and bring that girl over to the front desk. "Put the other two girls in the patrol car," Dan said.

Jorge Manuel and one of the policemen escorted the other two girls outside. Don Fernando and the tall blonde and two other policemen stood in front of Dan. The tall blonde was still yelling that she wanted a lawyer. Dan gave her a quick cold look. He thought of Mumbai. He wondered what her name was. He remembered there were at least three bottles of ayahuasca still left in his refrigerator from before don Fernando had taken him to see Dr. Cruz. Still in his refrigerator... waiting for him.

"You can uncuff her," Dan said.

The blonde stopped yelling and looked at Dan

"But Dani..." don Fernando started to say.

"It's okay," Dan said.

Don Fernando uncuffed her.

She rubbed her wrists and said to Dan, "Thank you, sir. That's more reasonable."

"You must be Violet," Dan said with a smile.

She seemed startled, but nodded her head and said, "It's pronounced Violeta, but yes."

"Don Fernando," Dan said, "can I borrow your gun?"

Don Fernando's eyes widened, but he unhooked his gun from the holster and handed it to Dan.

Dan held the gun in his hand and looked at it, turning it slowly. Violeta looked at it too.

Then Dan jammed it into her stomach.

"Violeta, I am going to blow you in two pieces if you don't tell me where Krasko is."

Don Fernando had never heard such a cold voice in all his life. He felt the hairs stiffen on the back of his neck. The two other policemen also seemed frozen in place.

Violeta's mouth was moving up and down but no sound came out. Finally she muttered, "I... I have rights..."

Dan took the gun out of her stomach and put it up by her head with the barrel pointing towards the ceiling and pulled the trigger. A huge bang filled the lobby. Violeta cringed and collapsed backwards into the arms of don Fernando and the other policemen. The desk clerk fell to his knees. What was left of tourists and gawkers in the lobby scattered towards the exit doors. Plaster fell from the ceiling.

Don Fernando and the police picked Violeta up and held her in front of Dan, maintaining a grip on her arms. She looked terrified.

"It's a farm house," she yelled, "outside of town."

"Draw a map, now!" Dan yelled, pointing to the paper and pen on the counter.

She reached over and picked up the pen with shaking hands and started to draw.

Dan stuck the gun in her back, and said, "And if you mislead us, I will personally come to your jail cell and blow your fucking brains out."

She drew faster, then handed the sheet to Dan. "No," she said, "This is accurate. I swear."

Dan looked at the map and nodded. Don Fernando re-cuffed her. The two policemen dragged her outside to the waiting patrol car.

Dan handed the pistol back to Don Fernando.

"Thanks," he said.

"Dani," don Fernando asked, "how did you know her name?"

A frown came over Dan's face. How *did* he know her name? He looked at don Fernando, shrugged his shoulders, and just said, "Ayahuasca told me."

"But Dani..."

"I don't know, don Fernando... I just knew it. Come on," he said, looking at the map, "Let's go get these guys."

*   *   *

Meanwhile, Krasko was still sitting by the front door waiting for Rune to get back.

"That incompetent little shit," Krasko thought to himself. "What's taking him so long? He just needed to stop at one store." Krasko was looking forward to killing Rune. He never had liked him. He had only tolerated him because Puii needed him.

Krasko was so busy thinking about how much he disliked Puii and Rune that he did not hear Rune sneaking up behind him.

"You left quite a mess in the hallway," Rune said.

Krasko twisted in the chair and half-rose before he realized that Rune was standing about ten feet from him... with a gun in his hand... aimed right at Krasko's chest. Krasko twitched towards his shoulder holster.

"Don't do that," Rune said firmly.

Krasko recognized the gun in Rune's hand. It was a Glock 41. It used .45 caliber bullets. Unlike his little .22 caliber, Krasko knew that one round from Rune's gun would be sufficient to kill him. Krasko's best bet was to bluff. He straightened up and smiled broadly.

"Rune, my friend, you startled me. I didn't hear you come in."

"Uh huh," said Rune, watching Krasko.

"Yes, I had to shoot Puii," Krasko explained, still smiling. "He was going to betray us, steal our product, and sell it to the Pakistanis."

"Yes," Rune said, "we know all about that."

Krasko stopped smiling. "We?"

"The Thai Armed Forces Security Center," said Rune. "We've been monitoring you, Puii, and Khambang for the past year."

Krasko couldn't believe what he was hearing. "What?" he said weakly.

"Yes," Rune continued, nodding his head, "and on behalf of the Royal Government of Thailand, the military, and the Thai people, I want to thank you for saving us the trouble of growing this tissue. And I want to personally thank you for saving me the trouble of killing Puii. There was no way we were going to let this material fall into Pakistani hands. No siree."

Krasko's mind was reeling. This could not be happening. He was going to retire after this delivery. He was going to be rich. The world was going to be his.

"Rune... my friend... everything that you and I have worked so hard for... This shipment is worth millions. Rune, we could both retire..."

"Yes, I know," Rune said. "This material is very valuable."

"What say we pack it up and take it to the airport now?" Krasko asked. "We can split the proceeds and both disappear."

"Yeah no, I don't think so," Rune said. "I don't think that's going to happen."

"Wha… What is going to happen now?' was all Krasko could think to say.

"Now? Well now I'm going to kill you," Rune said, and pulled the trigger.

The force from the Glock's bullet knocked Krasko's body backwards. He slammed into the open front door and slid to the floor. Blood seeped out of the huge hole in the middle of his chest and slowly turned his shirt deep red.

Rune slid his Glock back into his holster and thought to himself, "Shit, now I have to clean up two bodies. What a mess! But first, I'll email Bangkok and tell them the material is ready to ship."

Chapter 15

*The best plans of mice and men
can come to a horrible end,
when greed takes control
and men lose their souls,
into hell fire they descend.*

Rune was beginning to type out his email to Bangkok when he suddenly heard cars coming up the driveway. He could tell it was more than one car. He jumped up and dashed out of the back room, pulling his Glock from its holster.

But he came to a dead stop in the living room. There, standing over the body of Krasko, were two uniformed policemen and three men in civilian clothes. All of the men, except one who looked like a gringo, had drawn their guns and were aiming them right at Rune.

But it was the gringo spoke first. "I would drop that gun if I were you."

Rune let the gun fall from his hand.

"And put your hands on the top of your head."

Rune complied.

Dan glanced at don Fernando, and pointed down to the lifeless body on the floor, "I recognize Krasko." Dan looked at Rune. This was not Puii. This was the other guy he had seen in his vision. "Where's Puii?" Dan said coldly.

Rune didn't know how this gringo knew Krasko's or Puii's name, but he said nothing.

Two policemen, also with guns drawn, appeared behind Rune.

"Capitán," one of them shouted. "There is a dead man in the hall back here."

"Ah," said Dan, "that answers that question."

One of the policemen behind Rune grabbed Rune's hands and pulled them behind Rune's back and put handcuffs on him.

Rune finally spoke, "Gentlemen, you cannot arrest me. I am a diplomat from the Thai government. I can show you my papers. I have diplomatic immunity."

"Fuck you and your diplomatic immunity," Dan said.

"Should we take him to the jail in Villa Rosario or the one in La Chorrera?" don Fernando asked Dan.

Dan scratched his head. Without ayahuasca to give him a view into the future, he wasn't sure what to do next. A quick image of Mumbai flickered across his mind.

"Neither," he said. "Hold him here until we sort a few things through. I want to see where the tissue is."

Two policemen grabbed Rune's arms and sat him down in a wooden chair and put a second set of handcuff through the first set, locking him to the chair. He glared at Dan as Dan walked down the hallway looking into the different rooms. Who was this gringo? How did they find him here? How did they know about the tissue?

Puii's body was splayed out in the hallway. Dan had to step over it carefully to avoid stepping in any blood.

"I'll call for an evidence technician, Dani, to take photos of everything," don Fernando said.

"Yeah... um not yet, don Fernando. "Let's just hold off on that a bit."

Don Fernando was puzzled. It was unlike Dani to not be always collecting and indexing evidence, he thought to himself.

Dan finally found the back bedroom. He opened the door and switched on the light. There were shelves of glass aquariums, all completely full of that gray matter.

"This is it," Dan muttered to himself. "The belly of the beast."

He stepped out of the room and gestured for Jorge Manuel and don Fernando to gather close around him.

He spoke to the two men in a low, but direct, whisper. "Look, amigos, I did not have time to tell you back in the restaurant all that I have learned... so I have to ask you to simply trust me on this." Dan looked at Jorge Manuel and said, "Jorge Manuel, I have been don Fernando's friend for ten years. I have never misled him. I have only known you a short while, but if you think back to that case last year, that murder in the bathhouse, you will remember, I never misled you, either."

Jorge Manuel nodded in agreement. Dan continued, looking at both men. "You have to trust me on this. I will explain it all later, but that *stuff* in those incubators, in those aquariums," he said gesturing to the shelves in the room behind him, "is so dangerous, so toxic... we must destroy it now. Don Fernando, my memory is that your patrol cars each carry a canister of gasoline in the trunk, right?"

Don Fernando nodded his head yes.

"Please trust me on this, don Fernando. Can you have your men bring a few of those to the back of the house?"

Don Fernando looked at Dan. Don Fernando had been the police chief of Villa Rosario for many decades, and he maintained that position by having a combination of great discretion, a intuitive sense of who he could trust, and how much he could bend the law. He knew Dan was going to bend the law, but he trusted Dan. He nodded his head yes and went to the front of the house to instruct his men.

Jorge Manuel, let's you and I go find some wood," Dan said.

Dan and Jorge Manuel went out back and found some lumber scraps on the side of the house. They threw them in a pile about 100 yards away from the house. Several policemen carried red canisters of gasoline to the back of the house and gave them to Dan.

Dan asked don Fernando to have his men carry each incubator carefully to the back and place them by the wooden pyre. Then he walked to the front room where Rune was still sitting handcuffed in the chair.

Don Fernando handed Dan Rune's passport that his officers had found while searching the other bedrooms.

Dan opened it and looked at it. He flipped through the pages and noted several visas stamps to India from Thailand.

"Doesn't exactly look like an diplomatic passport," he said to Rune.

"I have papers!" Rune spit out.

"I bet you do," Dan said. "Tell me... Rune... were you with Puii and Khambang in Mumbai when they injected those homeless men with the early versions of the pig tissue?"

Rune's eyes widened. How *much* did these people know? he wondered.

"Yeah, I thought so," Dan said. "I suppose that's part of a diplomat's job, isn't it? Killing homeless people in Mumbai so you could develop a new type of soldier?"

Then Dan said to the two policemen guarding Rune, "Bring him and the chair out back please."

The two policemen unshackled Rune from the chair and dragged him and the wooden chair out to the back of the farmhouse.

"Sit him next to the wood," Dan said.

They sat Rune back down in the chair and re-shackled his handcuffs to the chair.

Jorge Manuel came out from the side of the house carrying several planks of lumber. "I found some more wood," he said.

"Good," Dan said. "The more the better."

When they finished stacking the lumber onto the pyre, it was about four feet tall and six feet wide. Jorge Manuel walked over and stood next to don Fernando and whispered, "Is this proper? Is this how they do it in the states?"

Don Fernando shrugged and said, "Well, Dani asked us to trust him, and we agreed, so let's just stand here and see what happens. He may be crazy, but maybe he's not..."

Dan started emptying the gasoline cans onto the wood.

Rune looked at the wood pile, at Dan pouring gasoline, and at the incubators on the ground in front of the wood pile.

"What are you doing?" he asked nervously.

"I'm going to burn all this tissue," Dan said calmly.

"No... no, you can't do that!" Rune exclaimed. "It's very important."

"Really?" Dan said. "Tell me."

Rune hesitated, and then said. "Look, I am not really an embassy diplomat. But I *am* a special agent for the Thai Armed Forces Security Center. I was sent here undercover to stop these men from delivering this tissue to the United States. I can prove this. I can give you the phone numbers to the Thai Security Center."

"Uh huh," Dan said, as he emptied another canister of gasoline onto the wood.

"Yes. This man Krasko was going to sell this product to the United States military," Rune said.

"Well actually," Dan corrected him, "he was going to sell it to Ravanco, and Ravanco was going to sell it to the U.S. military."

"Well, yes... yes, that's true," Rune said, "but I wasn't going to let that happen."

"Right," Dan said. "You were going to kill both Krasko and Puii and take the tissue back to Thailand."

Rune started sputtering. "Well, well, if I had to kill them, it would only be to keep this material from falling into the wrong hands."

"The wrong hands!" Dan shouted. "You were going to give it to the Thai military! How are their hands any cleaner than the U.S. military's?"

Rune mouth opened but he couldn't think of anything to say.

Dan threw a match on the wood. There was a giant whoosh and flames erupted to the sky. The heat was so intense that Rune had to turn his head away from the flames. Dan bent down and picked up one of the incubators and threw it onto the pyre. The glass shattered as the fire consumed it. The tissue sizzled as the fire incinerated it into black charred husks. Dan gestured to two policemen standing there to throw the rest of the incubators into the fire. They started heaving the incubators into the flames.

"You don't know what you're doing!" Rune shouted.

"Oh yes I do!" Dan answered back. "You know what this stuff produces—it produces soldiers! Pig soldiers! Cannibal soldiers!"

"I know!" Rune shouted over the flames and breaking glass. "But do you think we were the only ones developing this? Every country is rushing to breed some new type of soldier. We were trying to prevent this stuff from going into production. We were trying to stop it!"

"Liar!" Dan shouted. "If you were trying to stop it, you could have stopped it in Thailand! You could have stopped it in Mumbai! You let it go on so they could perfect the technique. You let go on so you could have the final product."

"We had to get it first, so we could prevent other countries from developing it! We were trying to contain it. We were trying to do good!"

"Good!??" Dan screamed in amazement. "By killing those men in Mumbai? By killing Khambang in that hotel? By killing those two hookers?"

"Collateral damage!" Rune screamed. "I'm burning up! Move me away from this fire!"

"Oh, you think it's hot now?" Dan yelled. He grabbed a piece of lumber and threw it on top of the burning pyre. "Tell me the truth, Rune—the Thai military wanted that tissue, didn't it? They sent you here with instructions to wait until the final product was ready to grow soldiers, didn't they? You were going to ship the tissue to Thailand and they were going to grow those soldiers, weren't they?

Rune rocked his chair so that he and the chair fell over to the ground, away from the fire.

"Yes!" he screamed. "Of course! It's a military weapon! It was developed in Thailand. It was ours! Of course we wanted it! We didn't trust the U.S. military with it—would you?"

"No, but neither would I trust your military with it!" Dan shouted.

The policemen threw the last of the incubators onto the huge bonfire. The glass exploded and the tissue sizzled.

Dan said to the two policemen, "Go back in the house and bring any equipment out, any vials, chemicals, boxes, anything with liquid in it, and throw it onto the fire."

Then he walked over to Rune, grabbed the back of the chair and picked the chair and Rune back up and sat him in front of the fire again.

"It's too hot!" Rune yelled.

"So tell me, Rune, how many people died in Mumbai?" Rune just shook his head no.

Dan pushed the chair an inch closer to the fire.

"Maybe a hundred, I don't know! There were many! But they were unknowns! They were expendable!" Rune shouted, turning his face away from the fire.

"And you helped Puii and Khambang do that," Dan said.

"I was undercover! I had to! There was no other way to catch them!"

"Stop lying!" Dan shouted. "You weren't trying to catch them! You were trying to help them grow this stuff! You were here to learn from Puii how to grow this stuff! And you did learn it, didn't you?"

Suddenly, the realization hit Dan. He stared at Rune.

"You're the only one who knows!" he shouted. "With Krasko and Puii dead, you're the only one who knows how to convert that red tissue into the pig tissue! Not only were you going to take the tissue back to Thailand, you were going to take the knowledge of how to make more back to Thailand, so that your military could grow as many soldiers as they wanted!"

Rune snarled at Dan. "Yes! I was! I am a soldier, doing what I was ordered to do!"

"Yeah..." Dan said, "me too." And he walked over and picked up the last gas can, the one that still had gasoline in it. He uncapped it, and walked over to Rune, and poured it all over Rune, dousing him, and then, as Rune started screaming, Dan kicked his chair into the fire.

Jorge Manuel gasped and started to move forward, but don Fernando grabbed his shoulders and spun him around. "Let it be, Koke!" don Fernando shouted.

Rune's body twisted and struggled as the flames ignited the gasoline, exploding and enveloping him in white hot flames, instantly turning his flesh black. Through the flames Dan could hear him screaming. One of the policemen turned and threw up. The other one just turned away. The smell of burning flesh filled the air.

In a few minutes, the intense fire consumed Rune and the chair. The outline of his body was twisted and fragmented, becoming one with the burning lumber and white-hot coals.

Dan walked over to the two uniformed policemen. "Did you get all the lab equipment and throw it on the fire?"

They both nodded, very afraid of this gringo.

"Okay," Dan said. "Go back inside and get any notebooks, any paper with writing on it, any computers, any thumb drives, any cell phones, anything that could have any kind of data on it and throw it on the fire."

The two policemen nodded and ran inside.

Dan walked over to where don Fernando and Jorge Manuel were standing.

"I'm sorry don Fernando... it had to be done. He knew how to make that tissue... Look, I have so much to tell you, but I am worn out... But listen, as soon as word gets out that these guys are dead, this house is going to be swarming with FBI, and agents from Thailand, and who knows what other countries. They're going to be looking for notes, computers, anything that would help them recreate that tissue. Your men have got to locate all of it and burn it... tonight."

Don Fernando nodded.

"If it were up to me, I'd burn the whole house down," Dan continued, "but it probably belongs to some old panameño with no insurance... You have to swear your men to secrecy, don Fernando."

"No worries, Dani. My men are loyal to me."

"Yeah, they're probably all relatives," Dan said.

Then Dan looked at Jorge Manuel. "Jorge Manuel, are any of your men here tonight?"

"No, Señor Landes. These are all don Fernando's officers."

"Well, when you get back to La Chorrera, your men may have questions, but you can't tell them *anything* that happened here."

Dan thought for a moment, then said, "We need to guard the fire until it burns out. Don't call the fire department. Let the fire burn out. We'll try and retrieve the handcuffs from the ashes if they haven't melted. Tell the newspapers that you came out to investigate the fire and discovered the two bodies in the house. Don't say anything about the guy in the fire. Just say someone killed both the people in the house. Make the FBI and the Thai government believe that Rune killed Krasko and Puii.

"Why not throw those two on the fire, too?" Jorge Manuel asked.

Dan and don Fernando turned and looked at him.

"Well, I mean, that way you don't have to explain anything," Jorge Manuel explained. "No bodies."

Dan and don Fernando looked at each other, then turned and stared at Jorge Manuel again.

"Sorry," Jorge Manuel said, "I was just trying to think... like a gringo."

"I like how you think," Dan said, then he looked at don Fernando again. "What do you think, don Fernando?"

"Well, his idea has merit," don Fernando said, rubbing his chin. "A lot less paperwork... and they're both extranjeros, so—and pardon me for saying this Dani—so nobody will care."

And so don Fernando nodded, and Dan nodded, and Jorge Manuel finally felt that he was making a contribution to the murder investigation, although he wasn't sure what it was. But the three men went into the house and dragged the bodies of Krasko and Puii out to the back yard. Don Fernando got another canister of gasoline from one of the patrol cars, and they doused the two bodies with gasoline and tossed them onto the fire. Once again the fire exploded and wrapped itself around the bodies.

Dan made a suggestion to don Fernando, and don Fernando agreed, and so don Fernando gathered his police officers in the front room while Dan and Jorge Manuel tended the fire. And don Fernando explained to the police officers that these three men were running an international drug ring; and that those aquariums contained a new and very lethal drug; and that the reason they were burning the bodies and all the drugs was to protect the officers; that if the Mafia were to discover that the men were dead, they would assume that the police killed them; and they would hunt down all the policemen who had been at the house or saw the men or saw the drugs, and kill them; but that this way, the Mafia wouldn't know the men were dead. They would just think that the men stole the drugs and fled Panama, and the policemen would be safe. And therefore, their lives depended on them not telling anyone what they had seen here tonight.

It's hard to say which was more effective in guaranteeing the policemen's secrecy—don Fernando's story or don Fernando's reputation. For don Fernando was correct when he told Dan that his men were loyal to him. But that was because they knew what he was capable of doing, and watching him help drag those bodies and burn them that night just reinforced their fear and loyalty to him. And so, they all pitched in and cleaned the house from top to bottom; mopping away the blood in the hallway and the blood in the front room; burning everything that might have belonged to Krasko, Puii, or Rune; and wiping the place clean of all fingerprints. One of the officers found Krasko's keys to the van, and they cleaned that as well. Don Fernando knew a repair shop in Villa Rosario that occasionally operated as an illegal chop shop. He would arrange for someone to take the van there and sell it to them. The money he would use to give his men bonuses...

By the time the sun came up the next morning, the fire was burned out. Dan retrieved the partially-melted handcuffs from the ashes. Don Fernando sent his officers home and told them to all take the day off. Dan and Jorge Manuel used shovels to bury the ashes. Don Fernando looked up at the morning sky.

"Looks like it might rain," he said.

"That would be good," Dan said. "Freshen things up."

"Are we ready to go?" don Fernando said.

"Yeah," Dan said. "Will you drop me off at home?"

"Of course, Dani."

"I need to sleep for a day, but let's get together

tomorrow. Maybe for lunch, and I'll connect all the dots for you," Dan said.

"If you come to La Chorrera, I will buy your lunch," Jorge Manuel said.

"Deal," Dan said. "Los Cuñados at noon?"

Both don Fernando and Jorge Manuel nodded yes.

A few sprinkles started to fall from the sky.

Chapter 16

*Now we come to the end of our story
with all its greed, blood, and glory.
And now that we're through,
here's a secret for you:
There's more here than just allegory.*

Don Fernando dropped Dan off at his apartment that morning, and Dan immediately climbed into bed and slept through the day. It was a deep, but troubling sleep, as his subconscious mind tried to reassemble everything that had happened over the past five weeks.

Somewhere around midnight, between midnight and one a.m., he was awakened by a knock on his door. At first, he thought he must have dreamed the sound, because he looked over at the clock by his bed and saw the hour. So he closed his eyes and tried to go back to sleep. But then the knock came again.

"What the fuck?" he thought to himself. "Who would be knocking at this hour?"

He dragged himself out of bed. Even after sleeping all day, his body felt trampled and exhausted. He just wanted more sleep. He opened the door.

It was Khambang... the badly decomposed body of Khambang... trembling like a skeletal scarecrow in the wind. Very little flesh was left, and what there was, was peeling off in putrefied hunks.

Dan was too startled, too unbelieving, too groggy, and too numb to move or react or even to feel anything. A few strands of jute still held what was left of the corpse's mouth sewn shut, but Dan clearly heard it say "Thank you"... and then the corpse simply dissolved into dust before his eyes and was blown away by the wind. Dan closed the door and walked over to the refrigerator and opened it. The full three plastic bottles of ayahuasca were still there. They had sat there since that morning when don Fernando had taken him over to see Dr. Cruz.

Dan pulled one of the bottles out and uncapped it and took a long drink. The sweet smoky liquid slid down his throat. He walked over to the bed and climbed in, and fell immediately to sleep.

* * *

Late the next morning Dan woke up feeling refreshed. "What a weird dream," he thought, recalling the image of Khambang at his door. He got up, used the bathroom, splashed water on his face and brushed his teeth.

Normally he made coffee first thing in the morning, and drank the first cup in bed—just to get enough caffeine inside him so that he could wake up—but this morning he felt energetic. He decided to take a shower and shave first, and then to make coffee.

He showered and hummed an old pop song from the eighties as he washed. Then he got out of the shower, dried off, and shaved.

After he got dressed, he went into the kitchen and opened the refrigerator, intending to get the plastic container where he kept his coffee. He reached for the bottom shelf where the coffee was, and grabbed the container, but then happened to look at the ayahuasca bottles. There were still three bottles, but only two were full. One obviously had a large gulpful missing.

Dan's body froze. He *did* take a drink of ayahuasca last night! It wasn't a dream! Or did he dream the part about Khambang and then wake up thinking it was real and then got out of bed and went to the kitchen to find the ayahuasca? He didn't know.

He stood up and put the coffee container by the coffee pot and closed the refrigerator door. Then he walked over to the front door and opened it. There was just his balcony and the vista from his balcony to the central valley below. He looked down at the patio tiles. Yes, there was a brown dust there... but it was always dusty in Panama. The road in front of his apartment was a dirt road. He looked over the valley, and then closed the door and walked back into the kitchen to make coffee.

While the coffee was brewing, he sat at his little desk and thought. *This* is what Dr. Cruz meant that morning, when they were waiting for don Fernando to come pick him up... Dr. Cruz had told him that even though the ayahuasca was out of his system, the visitors still existed on the other side of the veil, but that the veil was stronger now, and even though it might be possible for a visitor to pierce the veil momentarily, they could never stay for long, and that he would not be scared again. Dr. Cruz had even said that many of his patients had gone back to using ayahuasca occasionally, but that Dan had to be careful, because ayahuasca is so seductive that it is easy to fall back into heavy use. During that conversation, Dan swore up and down to Dr. Cruz that he would never touch a drop of that liquid again... and yet... and yet he had kept the three bottles and had not thrown them away.

Dan poured himself a cup of coffee and thought about these things. Then he thought about what he would say to don Fernando and to Jorge Manuel at lunch. He also reminded himself that he owed Ricardo a lunch for telling them about the three blonde girls at the hotel in Villa Rosario. How was it, he asked himself, that sometimes fate seems to cause certain things to transpire... like Ricardo happening to come to El Balcón that particular day when Dan and Jorge Manuel and don Fernando were all there discussing Khambang's murder and those three blonde prostitutes? And how was it that Ricardo even knew where the three girls were? He needed to ask him that in some detail the next time he saw him, maybe when he bought him lunch... But what serendipity! For Ricardo to have had that information and to have shared that with them... or was it fate? Did the "visitors", as Dr. Cruz called them, actually influence things from the other side of the veil? Are we really all just totally in the dark on this side? Dan could never find the explanation of how he knew Violeta's name... He never really understood how it was that the ghost of Khambang seemed to give him clues all along... He had always assumed it was ayahuasca, but maybe not... Maybe ayahuasca was just a small tool that scraped the fog off the window between this side and the other side... Maybe the other side is the light and we all live in the dark...

Dan shook his head. He just didn't know. He looked at his watch. He had enough time for one more cup of coffee before don Fernando would come and pick him up to drive him to La Chorrera for that lunch. He needed to think about what he was going to tell them over lunch.

* * *

While Dan was pouring his second cup of coffee, Jorge Manuel was sitting at his desk, talking with his sergeant. He was explaining to the sergeant—in a very guarded way—what the outcome of the case was. Jorge Manuel and his uncle had decided to adopt Dan's suggestion about claiming the case was a drug cartel case.

"So dead man in the hotel was the courier, bringing drugs into Panama in the ice chest," Jorge Manuel was saying to the sergeant. "They had devised a way to cover the smell of the drugs with animal tissue, especially blood. They had forged documents saying they were bringing in organs for transplant in Panamanian hospitals so they could clear customs. The courier delivered the drugs to the other three men, and those three men then transported it into the United States."

"I see," said the sergeant. "And why did they kill the man in the hotel?"

"I don't know, sergeant. Maybe a disagreement over payment, or maybe the courier had diluted the drugs... who knows? Murders in the drug trade are, as you know, very common."

The sergeant nodded. "And the gringo and the two Asians—they escaped?"

"We think the American authorities must have picked

181

them up. We know the FBI had the under surveillance. Don Fernando says they made it as far as the airport in Miami when they were all three arrested."

"Ah, good," the sergeant said. "Then, our work is done?"

"Yes," said Jorge Manuel. "There's nothing more for us to do. Thank you, sergeant, for all your good work on this case. Let us hope we have a murder-free week this week."

"Sí, capitán," the sergeant said as he stood up to leave.

"Oh, one more question," the sergeant said.

"Yes?"

"What shall we do with the Colombian girls?"

"Oh, yes," Jorge Manuel said. "Well, I guess we can release them. Tell them that the gringo and two Asians have been arrested in the states. And tell them that if they agree not to tell anyone about this case, we will keep their names out of any information we provide to the FBI about our investigation. I'm sure they would not want those criminals to know how they helped us."

The sergeant laughed. "Sí, capitán... Oh, and what happened to the three blonde prostitutes that were arrested in Villa Rosario. Were they released?"

"No, don Fernando is having them deported."

"Ah, too bad," the sergeant said. "I heard they were pretty."

Jorge Manuel just nodded. The sergeant saluted and left the office.

Jorge Manuel thought to himself: too bad pretty doesn't always help you... or being smart... It was clear to Jorge Manuel that the Khambang man and the man named Puii must have been very educated scientists... and that didn't save them.

Jorge Manuel leaned back in his chair and thought about the case, about all the murders, the prostitutes, what Dr. Vargas had explained about the pig-human tissue... He shook his head and thought that he needed to start going to church more often. At least he understood that.

* * *

At that same moment, Ricardo was sitting at his writing desk in Villa Rosario. He was not thinking about

182

Khambang or the three blonde prostitutes or the meaning of life. He was thinking of young Marco. He had always been very fond of Marco, even though he knew that their relationship had been built on the free meals and vacations that he treated Marco to. Well, at least now he had an excuse to visit the Hotel de Cero again, to update Marco on what Dan had told him—that neither Marco nor the hotel was under any cloud of suspicion. With the excuse of conveying that news, perhaps Ricardo could entice Marco to another lunch together. And maybe over lunch, he could suggest a small vacation together, to some discrete beach hotel for a night or two, some place small and out of the way.

Ricardo got up and went to look in the bathroom mirror. He was old. His hair and beard were almost completely white. He went back to his desk and sat down. He would maybe suggest a nicer hotel to young Marco, maybe a resort with a swimming pool and hang gliding and a casino. Maybe at his age, he needed to sweeten the pot a bit.

*　*　*

"First of all, I want to thank you both for trusting me the other night." Dan was speaking to don Fernando and Jorge Manuel. Miguel had seated them in the private room at the back of Los Cuñados at Jorge Manuel's request. They had all ordered their lunch, and Miguel had left the room.

"As I promised," Dan continued, "I want to explain the background of this case, so that you will understand how important it was... so that you will understand—and hopefully forgive—why I did what I did the other night... and that you will understand... well, let's just call it the bigger implications of this case.

"Over the past forty years, the world has become a much more dangerous place. Men have always fought wars, but the nature of war has changed. Many people hoped that the nuclear bomb would put an end to war—somehow that mutually assured destruction meant that neither side would risk war. But evidently, man's desire to kill each other is stronger than the risk of utter destruction, and so war simply evolved. Terrorism grew. And it grew because you can't bomb an anonymous enemy. You can't bomb a whole city kill one terrorist. So, in response, total surveillance grew. Drones were developed. In war, as in all other forms of nature, there is a balance of power. You develop a strength, and your enemy develops a counter-strength. Predators hunt; and so their prey learn to camouflage or elude. But man is evil, and is always trying to stack the deck, always trying to gain the killing advantage—better bullets, better tanks, poison gas, concentration camps, atomic bombs, laser bombs, drone bombs...

"But these guys took it to a whole new level. Bombs don't win the war on terrorism—you need soldiers on the ground to fight terrorists. But the public doesn't like the old image of war, at least not the American public. They don't want their sons coming home from war hooked on drugs, or suffering from PTSD, or being double amputees. And the terrorists know this. That's why they love to capture and then execute soldiers on video and send those images throughout the world via the internet. Executing one soldier on video is more valuable than winning an entire battle. No parent wants to see their sons or daughters executed, and all parents sympathize with that feeling.

"So, to offset this terrorist advantage, this company Ravanco came up with an idea: instead of using drone airplanes—which are basically robot airplanes—they had the idea of using robot soldiers. They were going to manufacture soldiers to fight these wars. So it wouldn't matter if one of them was captured and executed because he wouldn't be anyone's son. But metal robots are costly. So they came up with the idea of simply breeding soldiers—making clones—modifying DNA to create a killing machine. They figured if they could grow soldiers in one year in a laboratory, they could create an inexpensive killing machine. This type of scientific experiments would not have been allowed in the United States, so they did it in Thailand, by simply bribing scientists and legislators. And when they were caught, they simply moved to Mumbai. And then, as they were experimenting with creating these genetically-engineered robot soldiers, they came up with the demented idea of modifying the DNA further to make them..."

Dan paused. He felt angry coming up in his throat. He took a sip of water and continued.

"To make them cannibal soldiers. These guys figured out a way to hardwire DNA by crossing it with pig DNA to not only grow superfast, but to drink blood and eat human flesh. Not only would these soldiers kill the enemy, they would eat their bodies. You wouldn't need to feed them in the field. You could just turn them loose on a city, and they would eat anyone they encountered.

"Dr. Vargas analyzed the DNA of the tissue sample that I gave her from the broken glass in Krasko's villa. There is no doubt in her mind that that tissue was embryonic tissue—millions of tiny babies in each of those incubators—literally. Each of those incubators we burned contained a million soldiers! All you had to do was add blood and they would grow. Drench them in blood for one year, and you had pig-soldiers, with no conscience, no independent reasoning, but enough intelligence to follow orders and loaded up with the desire to just kill and eat other human beings whether they were enemy soldiers or civilians.

"If a military unleashed those creatures, they would wipe out anything in their path. And it wouldn't matter how many of these pig soldiers the enemy killed—they were cheap to produce! A military could grow another few million in one year! Cost nothing to feed in the field! Whoever controlled those cannibal pig soldiers would control the world.

"So... Ravanco saw the opportunity for tremendous profit. They were going to develop this process, perfect it, and sell it the product to the U.S. government. And they didn't care who they bribed... or killed... to get it done. Krasko was the perfect man for them. He controlled Khambang and Puii. And they almost got away with it.

"But... the Thai government figured out that something was up. Somehow they put the pieces together, but rather than expose it, they decided to simply monitor it, to infiltrate it... so they sent in this guy Rune. Rune was a soldier with a science background, and they arranged somehow for him to apply to Puii to be an assistant, and Puii hired him, and then eventually Ravanco hired him.

"And why did the Thai military send Rune? Because they were going to steal it and then *they* would be the most powerful country in the world..."

Dan shook his head.

"Everyone wants to rule the world," Dan continued. "But with this stuff, they could... Now, how the FBI found out, I don't know. And I should say, I don't even know *if* they found out. We don't know what they know, because they wouldn't tell us anything. Why they wanted Khambang's body, I don't know. I have a clue, a suspicion, but I don't know for a fact. But my suspicion is that Khambang's body was part of the process. That somehow, he altered his own DNA—how, I don't know—but that it was altered to form the base of the process. Maybe he was egocentric, or maybe he figured that it would make him indispensable to Ravanco. But he engineered it so that his DNA had to be the DNA that was used to create the pig-soldiers. But we'll never know.

"But we do know this, gentlemen: that no one has the complete process. Only Khambang, Puii, and Rune knew the formula... and they're dead. The FBI has Khambang's body, but they don't have the formula. Ravanco has the tissue that was made from Khambang's DNA, but they don't know how to convert that into the final product. I'm not saying we stopped this process... I'm not saying that we prevented someone from figuring out how to make something similar... but I am saying we slowed them down. Thanks to Jorge Manuel's excellent suggestion, everyone will now assume that Krasko, Puii, and Rune have disappeared with the tissue. I don't think anyone knows that they rented the farmhouse in Villa Rosario, so they won't even know where to look."

Dan looked at Jorge Manuel and said, "But I do suspect that in a few weeks, when everyone realizes that these guys have disappeared, that the FBI will be contacting you, and that you'll see an influx of Thai tourists asking questions, trying to get cozy with you or your officers. Or maybe that fellow in the Thai embassy will suddenly start acting friendly. Luckily, you can point to your faxes with the FBI and tell them that per their instructions, you have closed the case. As for any Thai tourists... I don't know. Maybe refer both the Thai embassy fellow and any tourists to the FBI. Your hands are clean. You don't know anything—that should be your story. Above all, never, ever mention Dr. Vargas or the police lab in Panama City. All you know is that some Thai man died in a hotel; the FBI faxed you that he was an American citizen; and they took the body. End of story."

Don Fernando and Jorge Manuel were nodding their heads in agreement.

"Are there any loose ends?" don Fernando asked.

"None that I can think of," Dan replied. "You'll have to tell your men to talk to no one about this case."

"Does Dr Vargas have any of that tissue left?" don Fernando asked.

"No," Dan said. "She destroyed it."

Just then the door opened and Miguel brought in a tray of food. He served plates to each of the three men and placed a new pitcher of water on their table.

Dan waited until after Miguel left the room before continuing.

"I think we should enjoy this lunch, and feel proud that we stopped these men, or maybe just feel lucky..."

Don Fernando and Jorge Manuel nodded in agreement.

"I'd like to say grace," Jorge Manuel said.

"I think that would be very appropriate," Dan said.

The three men bowed their heads and Jorge Manuel began.

"Oh heavenly father..."

-FIN-

www.ingramcontent.com/pod-product-compliance
Lightning Source LLC
Chambersburg PA
CBHW070952120726
47910CB00004B/1205